SUPERNATURAL.

THE UNHOLY CAUSE

ALSO AVAILABLE FROM TITAN BOOKS:

SUPERNATURAL™
THE UNHOLY CAUSE

JOE SCHREIBER

Based on the hit CW series SUPERNATURAL created by Eric Kripke

TITAN BOOKS

Supernatural: The Unholy Cause
ISBN: 9781848565289

Published by
Titan Books
A division of Titan Publishing Group Ltd
144 Southwark St
London
SE1 0UP

First edition April 2010
10 9 8

Visit our website: www.titanbooks.com

Did you enjoy this book? We love to hear from our readers. Please email
us at readerfeedback@titanemail.com or write to us at Reader Feedback
at the above address.

To receive advance information, news, competitions, and exclusive Titan
offers online, please register as a member by clicking the "sign up" button
on our website: www.titanbooks.com

A CIP catalogue record for this title is available from the British Library.

Printed and bound in the United States.

For my brother Dan

ON FAME'S ETERNAL CAMPING GROUND
THEIR SILENT TENTS ARE SPREAD AND
GLORY GUARDS WITH SOLEMN ROUND
THE BIVOUACS OF THE DEAD.

- Plaque at Gettysburg

ONE

Beauchamp was ready to die.

He stood at the top of the hill, staring down the wide green slope to the creek, silent in the midday heat. The birds had fallen quiet in the live oaks, and even the breeze had gone still, creating a deep, expectant hush that enveloped the entire field below. The world seemed to be holding its breath.

Then he saw them—soldiers in blue lining up along the rocky rampart on the other side of the creek. Even from this distance Beauchamp could see their muskets and the buttons on their uniforms glinting in the sun.

A moment later, they attacked.

Beauchamp didn't think. He charged full-tilt down the hill toward the high grass along the creek. His vision jostled, jerking up and down and side-to-side with the force of his own velocity. He could see the muddy creek water now, glinting through the reeds like broken glass. Grasshoppers and tiny insects flew out of the path of his boots. His legs felt as if they had detached from him, pinioning forward hard and fast, gobbling up swathes of the uneven field in long, hungry strides.

Behind him, there was a roar as his men launched themselves over the hilltop and followed him in his headlong charge.

Down below, Union riflemen rose up and fired from the other side of the embankment, the cracks of their guns sounding like heavy books being dropped on a library floor.

Then he was in the middle of it.

Beauchamp's own soldiers began firing back, running while they were shooting, stopping only to reload or when minie balls found them and pitched them permanently to the ground with unuttered cries of pain still lodged in their throats. Men were screaming now, letting out the Rebel yell or shrieks of agony.

Often it was hard to tell one from the other.

He sprinted the final few feet to the bottom of the hill. Breathing hard, staggering a little, he slowed his step until he was trotting, and then came to a complete halt in the middle of the clearing. All around him, his men were skirmishing hard and close, engaging the enemy on either side, filling his peripheral vision with the blurring, grunting work of hand-to-hand combat. A soldier flew past him and hit the ground, clutching his chest.

Beauchamp flicked the sweat from his eyes, focusing all his attention on one of the Union sharpshooters who stood behind the ridge, not twenty yards away.

He felt himself going absolutely still. Time seemed to freeze in its traces. He could smell the dust and gunpowder now, the cypress trees and the slow muddy odor of the creek, the smoke, sweat, and horses and coppery fresh blood, everything heightened to an almost agonizing degree. Everything else—the orders he'd been given, the town below that they were sworn to defend, the lives of the men around him—disappeared.

Even the sounds of battle dropped away until all he could hear was the pounding of his own heart.

The sharpshooter was a farm kid not much older than Beauchamp himself. He could see the Yankee's musket, a .58 caliber Springfield like his own, pointing right at him. He saw the rifleman relax a little, confidence easing into the kid's face as he drew a bead on his target. From this distance it would be almost impossible to miss.

Crack!

That was the Yankee's musket, accompanied by the muzzle flash bright in the midday heat. Beauchamp saw the little puff of smoke drifting upward.

Smiling, he waited for it…

And felt nothing.

The Union soldier blinked, waiting for him to fall. Still smiling, Beauchamp reached down to pull out his bayonet. It was sharp enough that he could see the honed bevel, and he admired the way it caught the light.

Do it. Do it now.

Working carefully, he drew the tip across his own wrist, cutting through the skin so that the blood dripped directly onto his musket, running down its barrel. Then he pointed it at the Union soldier, drew in a breath, letting it out and squeezing the trigger at the same time.

The musket kicked hard against his shoulder, and the bluecoat's head disappeared in a cloud of blood and skull fragments, his entire body blown backward by the force of the shot.

Beauchamp breathed.

Time broke and began to flow forward again. The sounds of the day returned. All around him, men were screaming—his men, the enemy's men, *all* the men in this insane, blood-choked world. It made Beauchamp feel dizzy and ecstatic and drunk at the same time, as the 32nd surged past him to overwhelm the Yankee rampart.

Beauchamp raised one hand and visored his eyes against the glaring sun. Up ahead, in the direction of Mission's Ridge, the Confederate flag was still flying high. Glimpsing it there, unfurled across the wide blue sky, he felt the walls of his throat tighten with emotion. He raised his musket again, but didn't reload.

Instead, he aimed the barrel outward. Somewhere to his left, one of his fellow soldiers, a private named Gamble, was staring at him, mouth half-open.

"What—" Gamble was struggling to breathe, "what happened?"

Beauchamp just grinned at him. He could feel the air

around his face vibrating a little, almost as if it was coming alive against his skin. The enigmatic majesty of the day was booming through him, like a shot of adrenaline straight to his neural plexus.

"I shot him."

"You *killed* him?"

Beauchamp's grin didn't falter.

"That's right," he answered.

"But how?"

"Easy as pie," Beauchamp said, and he turned the bloody musket around so that the bayonet was pointed straight at the private's disbelieving face. With a thrust, he shoved the blade straight into Gamble's right eye.

The private screamed, but it didn't sound like a Rebel yell anymore—it was a yodeling squeal of pain and terror.

Like the noise a suckling pig makes beneath the butcher's cleaver, Beauchamp mused.

Gamble collapsed, cupping his eyes, blood pouring through his fingers, and rolled onto his side. Beauchamp rammed the bayonet between his ribs, rolled him over, and stabbed him in the heart.

Silence.

Beauchamp looked up.

A hush had swept across the open field again. There wasn't even so much as a whisper of breeze. All around him, on both sides of the barricade, men had lowered their weapons and were staring at him with expressions of sheer disbelief. It was as if God—or some other deity—had pulled the plug on the entire enterprise.

From where he stood, alone in the open field, Beauchamp looked past the rampart to the sawhorses that divided the field from the parking lot where rows of cars and RVs and motorcycles glinted in the sun. Spectators—men and women and kids—were all gaping at him. Some of them turned away, covering their children's eyes.

A radio played tinny music. He could hear a woman's voice, very clearly.

"That's real blood, ain't it?"

"Dave...?"

Another man in a Confederate uniform and slouch cap came jogging toward him, haversack slapping against his left hip. He stopped when he saw Beauchamp standing over the bleeding corpse of Gamble at his feet. His face looked pale, and for a second he couldn't even speak.

"Dave. Jesus. Dude... what did you *do*?"

Beauchamp twisted his head around. He grinned again, placing the tip of the bayonet under his own chin, feeling the sharp tip against the soft part of the flesh.

"War is hell," he said, and he shoved the blade upward.

TWO

Sam Winchester was dreaming.

He dreamt he was standing in front of a picture window in a high-roller's suite at the Bellagio, with all the gaudy lights of Vegas spilled out below him like a handful of cheap jewelry.

Behind him, a smooth voice on the flat-screen plasma TV was giving him instructions for blackjack, an in-room tutorial that played twenty-four-seven on this particular channel.

Sam wasn't listening.

Somehow, in the dream he understood that he'd come here to gamble and that he'd won—won big. Turning around, he saw piles of chips and cash heaped on the unmade bed next to an empty champagne bottle that nestled in a chrome bucket full of half-melted ice.

The voice on the TV droned on in the easy, mellifluous manner of a lounge magician's patter.

"When the player chooses to double-down, it always

behooves him to look at the dealer's card first, and then his own."

The voice changed, brightening a little.

"How about you, Sam? Do *you* know what the dealer's holding?"

Sam glanced up at the screen. The face he saw there was familiar, from other dreams and nightmares through which he'd been suffering every night.

Lucifer.

"Sam?"

"Go away," Sam said. His voice was pinched tight. A feeling of tension was gathering around his throat, hot friction taut against his skin, constricting his vocal cords. "Leave me alone."

"Afraid I can't do that, Sam," Lucifer replied. "Not now. Not ever."

Sam tried to respond, but this time nothing came out. He couldn't even breathe.

"Look at yourself," Lucifer said, and then he was standing next to Sam. "Take a good long look in the mirror and tell me what you see."

Look at himself? That was easy. There was no shortage of mirrors in the suite.

He turned to the nearest one, fingers already clutching for whatever was tightening around his neck. But all he could detect in the mirror was a faint rippling of the skin around his throat.

Behind him, Lucifer started laughing.

"You won't remember most of this when you wake up,"

he said, almost sympathetically. "But you'll know that I'm coming for you."

Sam still couldn't speak. Deep bruise-colored marks were appearing like a collar around his neck. He saw them darkening, forming like the imprints of invisible hands.

Fear—panic—sprung up in his belly like a cold spike.

He wanted to scream.

Somehow he understood that if he could just manage to make a noise, it would stop. The marks would vanish and he'd be able to breathe again.

But he couldn't.

And he *couldn't.*

And he—

"Hey! Hey, Sam. *Drooler.*" There was a hand, shaking him, and none too gently. "Yo! Wake up."

Sam grunted, jerked backward and opened his eyes, lifting his head away from the window. Behind the wheel of the Impala, Dean regarded him with a look of brotherly amusement.

"Wipe your face off, man, you look like a freakin' glazed donut."

Without saying a word, Sam grabbed the rearview mirror and tilted it down, lifting his chin to look at his neck. It was unblemished, the skin normal. He let out a breath and sank back into his seat, feeling more wrung-out than relieved.

Dean glanced over at him again, his expression carefully neutral.

"Bad dream?"

"You could say that." Sam could feel Dean waiting for more, but the imagery was already starting to fade, leaving only a nebulous sense of dread. Trying to articulate it now would only make his brother more suspicious. "Anyway, I'm fine."

"Yeah?" Dean didn't sound convinced.

"Yeah."

"Good." That was that.

Dean reached down to turn up the radio, where Lynyrd Skynyrd was trucking through one of the final iterations of 'Sweet Home Alabama.' The song had played twice in the last half-hour, but Dean dialed it up anyway, filling the silence with guitars and drums.

Sam found a fairly clean fast food napkin on the floor and wiped the corner of his mouth, then balled it up and peered out of the window at the scenery. Georgia pines and scrub oak flashed by—heavy forest. Beyond it lay miles of swampland interrupted only by the occasional plantation house, creeks, and hills—the same terrain that had challenged the soldiers of the North and South almost a hundred and fifty years earlier.

"How much further?" he asked.

"Shush, I love this part." Dean turned the guitar solo up, lost in the moment, then came out of it. "Sorry, what'd you say?"

"You do realize we're not in Alabama, right?"

"None of Skynyrd was from there, either." Dean shrugged. "But you know where they recorded the song?"

"Let me guess—Georgia?"

Twenty minutes later they arrived at the cemetery.

* * *

The state police had cordoned off the front gates to keep the TV reporters out, along with what looked like at least a hundred curious onlookers. Some held homemade signs: "Cemetery Boy, We Love You" and "Come Home, Toby." Driving through the crowd, Dean reached out of the window and flashed an FBI badge, and a trooper waved them through with the tired expression of an official long since exhausted with his duties.

Sam didn't blame him. It was a zoo out there.

The graveyard itself was a sprawling old stretch of moss-covered swampland, dotted with ancient gray headstones, many of which sloped sideways or had fallen over, disappearing into the soft earth. The names had disappeared completely off many of the stones, leaving only smooth amnesiac marble.

Dean parked the Impala under a tall oak tree and he and Sam climbed out, wearing ill-fitting suits that clung to them in the heat. They walked toward the police cruisers and blue uniforms clustered a hundred yards ahead.

"So," Dean said, "this kid, Cemetery Boy..."

"Toby Gamble," Sam said.

"Four days ago he disappears from the house."

"Right."

"Nobody sees a thing."

"As far as I know."

"And then, yesterday morning..."

They stopped in front of the mausoleum where a few of the cops were gathered, drinking coffee. Most were staring at the words that had been scrawled directly on the stone in childish, dark reddish-brown letters.

HALP ME

"Kid isn't much of a speller," Dean commented.

"He's only five."

"Probably a product of home-schooling."

"So are we." Sam checked the pages he'd printed out earlier. "His mom confirmed that it's his handwriting."

"And the blood?"

"Sample's still at the lab."

"So that's all we got?"

"That," Sam said, "and this."

He pointed over the hill. Dean looked at the headstones that stood on the western edge of the cemetery.

"Oh."

The stones, dozens of them, were all splattered and streaked with the same crooked, spidery childish handwriting.

HALP ME HALP ME HALP ME HALP ME HALP ME

Dean nodded.

"At least he's consistent."

"His mother says she heard voices in his room the night before he disappeared."

"What kind of voices exactly?"

"We can ask." Sam turned and glanced back at a blonde woman who was standing next to the police. She was in her early twenties, but thin and tired in a way that made her look at least two decades older. It was easy to imagine her waiting tables on a Saturday night, bussing trays of empty bottles and getting pinched by drunken patrons while the jukebox yodeled out this month's country anthem.

Moving closer, Sam could see that she was holding what looked like a pale blue rag, wringing it in her hands and clutching it to her chest. After a moment he realized it was a child's t-shirt.

"I just want him back," she was saying, her voice thick with barely-contained emotion. "I just want my boy back."

"Ma'am?" Dean asked, stepping up next to her.

She jerked her head up, startled and red-eyed. The cop she had been talking to eyed them warily.

"Yes?"

"I'm Agent Townes, this is Agent Van Zandt, FBI. We were wondering if we could ask you a few questions about your son."

"I've already talked to the police."

"This will only take a minute."

"I don't... I'm sorry... I just don't know if I can..."

"The voices you heard in your son's bedroom," Dean persisted, "what were they saying?"

"It was... words, some language I didn't understand. Then they just kept saying his name. At first..." new tears began to well up in her eyes, "I just thought it was the TV. Then I heard him scream. I ran inside, but he was already gone."

She shook her head, pale blue eyes flashing out over the cemetery, and held the t-shirt closer to her chest.

"When I heard about all of this, I thought..."

There was a sudden shriek from across the graveyard, and Sam and Dean spun around, searching for the source of the noise.

An African-American man was walking from between the tombstones, and he was carrying a young boy in his arms. The child's entire upper body was splashed and splattered with scarlet, but he was alive, squirming in the man's grip.

"You!" one of the cops shouted. "Freeze! Drop the boy, now!" He pulled his pistol and aimed it at the newcomer.

Sam scowled.

"Is that...?"

"*Rufus?*" Dean blinked. "What the hell...?"

Dean and Sam stepped toward their fellow hunter. The jittery policeman lowered his gun, puzzled by their familiarity with the apparently blood-soaked stranger.

Rufus Turner stopped and released the boy, who immediately ran over to his mother.

"It's okay," Rufus said, and he glanced down at his jacket. It too, was covered with red. "Except for the damn karo syrup all over my clothes."

"Karo syrup?"

"Kid had a whole bottle of it stashed behind the trees over there."

The boy was talking now. Though he was speaking in a low tone, his words were clear.

"Mommy, I don't want to play this game anymore," he said, hugging his mother—who suddenly looked as though she didn't want to be anywhere near here. "I'm hungry, and my stomach feels funny."

Then, abruptly, he threw up.

"Swell," Dean muttered, and he cast a glance at Rufus. "I didn't know you were on this one already."

Rufus shrugged.

"I was in the neighborhood, headed over to the town of Mission's Ridge. Thought I might stop in here first and see what's what. Now my last clean shirt looks like somebody did heart surgery in it."

"Sir, we've got some questions," one of the plainclothes detectives said. "Would you mind coming with us?"

"You gonna pay my dry cleaning bill?" Rufus asked.

Sam glanced up.

"What's the Mission's Ridge thing?"

"Shooting during a Civil War re-enactment," Rufus said quietly. "Couple of civilians died."

"So?"

"The guns were replicas." Rufus looked at them. "And they were covered in blood."

"*Real* blood this time?"

"That's what I heard."

"That's it?" Dean asked. "Where d'you hear about it?"

"Anonymous email tip. Source up in Maryland of all places."

Dean scowled.

"Maryland?"

"Place called Ilchester. Why, have you heard of it?"

Dean turned to Sam, who was already staring at him.

"Who was your source?"

"I told you. Anonymous."

"Then we'll take that one," Dean said. "Give us whatever you've got, and we'll work it."

"You sure? Why are you so interested?" Rufus asked.

"Forget it," Dean said. "You go get your jacket cleaned."

THREE

An hour later Dean took one hand off the wheel and pointed at the sign that stood on the right side of the two-lane highway.

WELCOME TO HISTORIC MISSION'S RIDGE,
GEORGIA, FRIENDLIEST LITTLE
TOWN IN THE SOUTH
"WE'RE DANG GLAD YOU'RE HERE!"

"See, I told'ya this was a good idea," Dean said. "They're *dang* glad."

Sam glanced up from the open laptop on his knees.

"Wonder if the victims of the massacre enjoyed that famous Southern hospitality, too," he said dryly.

"Hey. So what's the Ilchester connection?" Dean asked.

Sam shook his head.

"Somebody wants us here."

"Or doesn't."

"Either way..."

"Let's call it what it is, Sammy," Dean said. "St. Mary's Convent in Ilchester, Maryland, is where you set Lucifer free. That's not a coincidence."

"I know." Not wanting to dwell on it, Sam turned his attention to the outskirts. Crossing a set of train tracks, they reached the center of town.

From their vantage point, Mission's Ridge consisted of a narrow main street with storefronts on both sides. Pedestrians milled around on the sidewalks, none of them in a hurry to get anywhere. Overhead, a banner announced the annual historical celebration and re-enactment of the Battle of Mission's Ridge. Whole families of curiosity-seekers wandered in and out of antique shops and cheap-looking museums advertising Civil War relics, moonlight ghost tours, and historical photos of you and your family in "genuine old time costumes."

None of them seemed particularly bothered by the recent shootings out on the battlefield.

They were driving through downtown proper now. Dean slowed down even more, finally easing the Impala to a stop. In front of them, a pair of tanned young women in denim cutoffs and halter-tops sauntered slowly by, one of them stopping and lowering her sunglasses to look in at Dean.

"On the other hand," he shook his head, smiling, "I do love the South."

Sam heard a wolf-whistle, and one of the women glanced up. From the other side of the street, two young Civil War soldiers in dusty Confederate uniforms and slouch caps walked in front of the Impala to meet the girls. The four of them stood in the intersection chatting, one of the girls reaching out to admire the soldiers' muskets.

"Hey!" Dean shouted out of the side window. "Mason and Dixon! War's over!"

The two soldiers ignored him. Dean blew the horn and one of the men raised an upturned finger in what Sam didn't think was a historically-accurate gesture. Slowly the quartet moved away.

"Come on." Sam couldn't help a smile. "Battlefield's on the other side of town."

"Right." Still the car remained where it sat.

"Dean."

"*What?*"

"Focus."

"I am, I am." He was still watching the girls and the soldiers in the side-view mirror. "Man, a job with travel is supposed to come with a *few* perks." Then he shrugged and turned to Sam. "Here, fix your tie, it's crooked." He reached over to help, and Sam flinched.

Dean frowned.

"What's going on?"

Sam hesitated.

"It's that dream I had earlier. I don't really remember much of it, except there was something around my throat, squeezing. And I couldn't breathe."

"That's it?"

"I think so."

Dean didn't look convinced, and Sam couldn't blame him. Nevertheless, he didn't remember the details, and any attempt to describe the vague feeling of dread would just make Dean even more on edge. If he *did* recall more—about the voice that had spoken to him, and what it had said—he'd share it.

Until then, he'd keep his silence.

Time to change the subject.

"On the bright side," he said, "at least we've got a wi-fi signal."

Turning back to the laptop, Sam scrolled through the various links his "Mission's Ridge" search had dredged up. There were ample references to the historic battle, and the town's annual re-enactment. But most of it was overshadowed by the previous day's reports of a Civil War re-enactor who had inexplicably managed to kill himself and two others with a replica musket and a bayonet no sharper than a butter knife.

The details matched what Rufus had told them back in the graveyard, with one notable exception: No mention was made of blood on the weapons.

"Looks like most of the fighting took place on a stretch of hillside along this creek, about two miles southeast of town," Sam said, pointing to a map on the screen. "That's where the re-enactors are camped now."

"And that's where the shooting took place?"

"Looks that way."

Dean tapped the accelerator, turned the radio back up, and eased them down the main drag.

A short time later he found the Allman Brothers playing 'Midnight Rider'—good solid Southern rock and roll—and turned it up, keeping the windows down to allow a breeze to flow through the car.

Soon they were out in the open countryside again, but the landscape was different now. The fields had been cleared, either by fire or real estate developers, and the grass was green, almost manicured. Sam could see monuments and cannons at the top of the next hill, along with rows of parked cars in a lot that seemed almost as big as the town they'd left behind. A large brown sign with bold white lettering stood on the right shoulder.

National Historic Site - No Relic Hunting.

"I'd say this is it," Dean said, and he pulled into the lot, crawling between the rows until he found an empty spot alongside a row of Harleys. All of the bikes had Confederate flags hanging from poles off the back. "You ready for action?"

Sam nodded and got out.

"According to the news reports, the shooter's name was Dave Wolverton. He was a waiter at a fast-food restaurant in Atlanta Airport. This was just a weekend thing for him."

"Yeah, well," Dean said, gesturing out beyond the parking lot, "he wasn't the only one."

As they reached high ground, Sam peered off to the west, and Dean saw a flicker of incredulity moving over his brother's face. Beyond the rows of spectators stretched a hillside that seemed to travel back, not just spatially, but into the recesses of time itself. Whole armies of men in blue and gray uniforms were bivouacked along both sides of the creek that ran along the bottom of the hill. There were tents and wagons, horses, fires and cannons, flags and farm implements sprawled out for what looked like hundreds of acres, as far as the eye could see.

"What do you think?" Sam asked.

Dean shook his head.

"I don't need *this* Civil War."

They cut a path through the rows of onlookers, past a row of Porta-Johns where long lines of people—a mixture of those in shorts and Kid Rock t-shirts, and others in historic clothing—waited to use the facilities.

Beyond that, the camps themselves took over. Soldiers milled around tents, admiring each other's weapons and uniforms. Women and children in similar attire moved through the crowds, and it seemed as if every conversation was filled with formalities the likes of which Dean hadn't heard since he'd dragged Sam to dinner at a Medieval Times theme restaurant.

The sounds of bugles and cannon-fire boomed from above.

"You hear that?"

"It's coming from up there," Sam said, pointing at the loudspeakers mounted along the periphery of the hillside. "The information online said they can even pipe in authentic battle sounds."

"Yeah," Dean said, "but where's the funnel cake?"

"This isn't a carnival, Dean."

"Come *on*. It's only history if you can eat it."

Sam just shook his head and kept walking.

"The news reports say Wolverton's unit was the 32nd."

They made their way along the hillside through crowds of re-enactors, looking for some sign that would identify Wolverton's group. Whether you could eat it or not, Dean thought, the gathering certainly bore one of the trappings of raw history; it didn't make a lot of sense down here on ground level. Maybe viewed from above, certain patterns would begin to emerge, but—

Suddenly he was knocked to one side.

"Hey," somebody snapped. "Watch where you're going, ass-hat."

The source of the comment was a burly, flush-faced Union soldier who looked as if he'd been enjoying far *too much* funnel cake, or whatever it was they served around the campfire.

Dean bristled.

"Excuse me?" he replied, planting his feet.

"Easy," Sam said, and he glanced at the soldier. "We're looking for the 32nd. Any chance you could steer us right?"

"Over that way," the man replied, still glaring at Dean. "Five or six tents over."

"Thanks," Sam replied, and he nudged Dean in the right direction.

"Ass-hat," Dean mused. "You think that's an authentic Civil War expression?"

Sam smiled. "Somehow I doubt it."

They walked deeper into the crowds of soldiers, past more tents and wagons. At one point Sam heard the clang of metal and looked over to see a muscular blacksmith bent over a forge, complete with an anvil and hot coals, banging out horseshoes, while a crowd of curious onlookers stood watching the sparks fly.

There was a railway shed next to the tree line, and off to their left, a makeshift corral of horses pushed their noses through the temporary wooden fence that had been set up to contain them. Delighted children held up apples and carrots for the animals to eat.

Finally, after wandering for another ten minutes, they came to a group of ten or twelve men in Confederate uniforms standing under a tattered canopy. One side of the tent was emblazoned with the identity of the group.

Fighting 32nd – Commanches

As they approached, the breeze changed direction and Dean caught a whiff of sour body-odor and unwashed hair, mixed with an acrid ammonia odor that he normally associated with drunk-tanks and nursing homes.

These guys are taking the whole authenticity thing a little too *seriously*, he thought to himself. A glance at his brother confirmed that Sam was thinking the same thing.

They stepped up next to one of the poles that supported the canvas.

"Fellas," he said.

The Confederates of the Fighting 32nd gazed back at him flatly, with such an utter lack of affect that they could have all been mannequins. Two of them were cleaning their muskets, while a third crouched in the midday heat, pouring water from a canteen over his neck and face.

Two others shied away from Sam and Dean completely, ducking behind the parchment map they held in their hands.

"I'm Federal Agent Townes," Dean pressed on. "This old boy is Agent Van Zandt. You guys soldiered with Dave Wolverton, didn't you?"

"That's right," the closest man said, shouldering his gun. He was a tall, gangly fellow with a thick Brillo-burst of unkempt red hair and a wispy attempt at a beard that ran down his neck and only exaggerated the size of his bulging Adam's apple.

"Were you there yesterday?" Dean asked.

The man nodded, and the look on his face said that he didn't really want to remember.

"Yeah, I was right behind him... maybe ten paces back during the charge." He stared off into the distance.

"So you saw what happened?"

"Yeah, I saw it." He turned back to Dean, then gestured to the others around the tent. "We all did."

"And we already talked to the sheriff." The other soldier

with a musket stepped forward. "Got nothing more to say."

Dean sized up the second guy, a brooding bear of a man with shoulders like barn-beams and eyebrows that seemed to have been applied with a Magic Marker. He appeared to take his role much more seriously, tilting his chin upward, as if daring them to challenge him.

Dean just shook his head, unwilling to take the bait.

"Stand down, Lieutenant," he said calmly. "Didn't mean anything by it. They're just questions."

"I'm a private," the bear growled. "Norwalk Benjamin Pettigrew, CSA, reporting for duty."

"Is that your real name," Sam asked, "or your...?"

"My what?"

"Your dress-up name," Dean finished.

"This isn't dress-up," Brillo-Head objected. "We're living historians. I'm Oren Henry Ashgrove. We're all re-interpreters. We—"

"My real name's Phil Oiler."

It was the bear-like man. Admitting the truth appeared to take some of the menace out of him, shrinking him a little in his uniform, and Dean actually found himself feeling a little sorry for the guy. "I sell life insurance in Atlanta."

"How well did you know Dave?"

"Oh, real well," Ashgrove said. "He's been with the 32nd for years. That's why what happened was so crazy. I mean, he was hardcore...."

"Hardcore how?" Sam asked.

"Every way imaginable," Oiler cut in. "He lost a ton

of weight, for one thing. During the war, your average Confederate soldier weighed 135 pounds. When he first joined up, Dave went on the Atkins diet for two solid years just to fit the profile. Stuck rocks in his boots. Shaved his face with a rusty piece of tin. You hear about his uniform?"

"Thrill me," Dean said.

"He was *totally* hardcore. The buttons... he soaked them in his own urine to properly oxidize the metal. He's the one that started all that."

"Hold up," Dean said, realizing now what the other smell he'd caught must have been. "You're saying you piss on your uniforms?"

"Not while we're wearing 'em. But yeah." The look of admiration on the large man's face was close to religious awe. "It's the only way to get the authentic look. I mean..." The respectful tone shifted to one of near-disgust. "you walk through here and see some of these farbs standing around checking their stock portfolios on their BlackBerrys. They dishonor the uniform, you know? Not Dave. He was just so..."

"Hardcore?" Sam finished.

"Totally."

"Hardcore enough that he might decide to bring a real gun to a historic re-enactment? Or a sharpened knife?"

The men shook their heads, but it seemed more like a gesture of disbelief than an actual answer—as if what Sam was suggesting was so sacrilegious that they lacked the words to respond.

"But you definitely saw him shooting?" Dean asked. "And

you saw the other soldiers get hit?"

Ashgrove said nothing, but Oiler managed a stiff nod.

"So the weapons *had* to be hot," Dean said. "Wolverton must have somehow modified the musket."

He waited.

"Right?"

Now neither man spoke.

"Where are the weapons now?"

Ashgrove shrugged.

"The sheriff's office, probably. Evidence."

"Was there any blood on the weapons?" Sam asked.

"There was blood everywhere."

"I mean, before Wolverton used them."

Ashgrove gaped at them, bewildered.

"Why *would* there be?"

Before Sam could come up with a response, another soldier—a tall, bald man who had obviously been listening in on the conversation—glanced up from behind the map.

"I think all the blood came after," he said.

Dean stepped toward him.

"And you are?"

The man stuck out his hand.

"Private Travis Wapshot, pleased to meet you."

"You're a part of Bad Company too?"

"The Commanches? Yeah, we're a pretty tightly knit group." Travis shrugged. "I guess it sounds crazy. And hell, I guess it probably is. But is it any nuttier than guys who drop ten grand in Vegas or run off for a wild weekend with their secretary?" He glanced at the grimy palms of his hands. "At least our dirt washes off."

"I don't know," Dean said. "That part with the secretary sounds pretty good to me."

Travis scowled.

"Beg your pardon?"

"Forget it. Let me ask you something. Why *do* you put yourselves through all this?"

The three soldiers exchanged a brief, unguarded look. Finally Travis responded.

"Sometimes modern life is too easy. We want to know what it was like for those guys back then. That was genuine experience, you know? The real thing." He paused in thought. "We had a guy in our unit, a pipe-fitter named Art Edwards, who died last year. Metastatic brain cancer. Ugly, drawn-out disease. But he trooped with us right up till his family put him in a hospice. He used to say his future didn't look too bright to him. He preferred the past."

"Maybe Dave Wolverton just got too fed up with the easy life," Sam said. "Decided to chuck it all."

The other two soldiers nodded soberly. It was hard to read their expressions.

"Can you think of anybody else who might be able to tell us about Dave?"

Travis nodded.

"You might want to talk to Will Tanner—he's a private in the 32nd. He and Dave palled around a lot, I think. Even outside of the Commanches."

"Is he here?"

"Haven't seen him. I'll see if I can dig up an email address, though."

Ashgrove spoke up.

"And they should meet up with the new guy..." he said, "the surgeon..."

"Oh, yeah!" Oiler cut in. "You *gotta* talk to the surgeon. He's *super* hardcore."

"Sure," Dean said. He'd had enough *hardcore*. "Well, hey, listen..."

"No, seriously! He's set up the medical tent right over beyond those trees." Oiler scowled. "He's got this totally cool name for himself, too—Doctor... what was it again?" He glanced around at the rest of the group.

Ashgrove thought for a second and snapped his fingers.

"Oh yeah. Doctor Castiel."

FOUR

The field hospital was nothing more than a stained canvas dog tent billowing in the breeze, fifty yards from the Commanches' bivouac. Even before Sam and Dean arrived, they could hear the groans and cries of the men laid out inside.

"Doc, I'm gutshot."

"It's bonebreak fever... I can hear the angel band calling me..."

"Gimme a bullet to bite on. This leg's got gangrene. I think it's gonna have to come off—"

To Sam—who had seen more than his share of pain and dying—the performances sounded unnervingly realistic.

Where did they learn to make it sound so convincing? he wondered. *And why would they* want *to?*

He lifted the tent-flap and peered in. Everywhere he looked, soldiers were scattered almost shoulder-to-shoulder on mats laid across the floor, or sprawled directly on the dirt.

Their groans and pleas were almost constant.

Standing in the middle of them, dressed in a shabby white coat that hung down to his knees, was the one man who looked even less like he belonged here than they did.

"Cass," Dean said. "What's going on? Why are you slumming with this crowd?"

Castiel didn't even look up. He had his hand on one of the wounded men's heads and his lips were moving slightly. Then he reached down and lifted the soldier upright, setting him on his feet and propelling him backward.

The re-enactor staggered away, nearly tripping over the bodies of the men behind him. Glaring with confusion, he looked up at Castiel.

"What the hell was *that*?"

"I've returned the strength to your legs," Castiel replied, his expression unreadable. Turning his back on the man, he opened his hands again. "Who's next?"

"Cass..." Dean started.

Still ignoring him, Castiel bent down over a soldier whose face was wrapped in layers of sagging, bloody bandages.

"Let me see," he said, peeling away the gauze and laying his hands directly over the man's eyes. "There. Now look upon me."

The re-enactor frowned, blinking.

"Where'd you come from, bro?"

"Heaven," Castiel said, and he began to lift the man's bloodstained shirt. "Now let me see that chest wound."

"Take your hands off me!" the man shouted, and he

squirmed away.

Castiel froze, his arms still partially extended. Sam shot Dean a look.

All around the tent, the other "wounded" had begun to pull back, withdrawing to the corners without completely abandoning the pretense of injury. Finally Castiel looked back and noticed that the Winchesters were standing there watching him.

A slight frown creased his forehead.

"Whoa," Dean said. "Awkward moment."

"What are you doing here?" Castiel asked.

Dean raised his eyebrows.

"Right back atcha, Cass."

"I walked the battlefields of the South a hundred and sixty years ago," Castiel replied, a faraway look entering his eyes. "I moved among the men and brought their souls to glory. And now..."

Something moved over his face for just an instant, so rare and brief that Dean almost didn't catch it: a flicker of hope.

"And now," he repeated, "I'm *healing* again."

"Cass..." Dean shook his head. "You do realize that none of these jokers is actually hurt, don't you?"

Castiel's expression darkened, but he didn't speak.

"See?" Dean nudged the man closest to him with his toe, and the re-enactor let out an authentic, well-rehearsed warble of pain. "It's a show. Their hobby. Like those couples that dress up in furry animal suits and..."

"Dean," Sam cut in.

"Sorry." He turned back to the crippled angel and shrugged.

Castiel regarded the tent around him again and sighed. He turned away, taking off the white coat and tossing it to the floor.

Still avoiding their eyes, he picked up his familiar trenchcoat from the back of a chair and slipped it on. When he turned to face Sam and Dean again, his face was utterly composed. The hopefulness was gone, buried beneath an iron mask of grim determination.

"I have more pressing business to attend to," he announced.

"The great God-hunt," Dean said. "Tell me, is He a Civil War buff?"

"I found a lead recently," Castiel announced. "A first-order witness."

"Is that like a mail-order bride?"

"First-order witnesses are among the rarest of celestial beings. The term refers to one who actually broke bread with Christ Himself."

"Six degrees of Jesus, huh?" Dean asked.

"Less than six. One."

"What makes you think he'll spill?"

"It is the break that I've been hoping for. Whoever the witness is, he will answer to me."

"Gotta respect the confidence," Dean said, "but let's face it..."

Then he stopped.

The place where Castiel had been standing was already empty.

Shaking his head, he looked around. Several of the re-enactors had broken character completely and were standing up, staring in disbelief at the spot where Castiel *wasn't*.

"Who *was* that freak?" one of them managed.

"*Freak?*" Dean looked around at them, grown men in costumes, huddled together with bruises and injuries painted on their faces, and Sam was afraid he was going to say something they'd both regret.

But he just shook his head.

"Don't worry about it," he said. "He won't be back."

FIVE

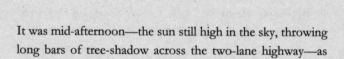

It was mid-afternoon—the sun still high in the sky, throwing long bars of tree-shadow across the two-lane highway—as Dean drove them back toward downtown Mission's Ridge.

"You think there's any connection between Castiel's Jesus witness and what's going on here in town?" Sam asked.

"How can there *not* be a connection?" Dean countered. "I mean, *The Passion of the Christ* isn't exactly on my Netflix list, but just because Cass's witness shared a Happy Meal with JC, it doesn't mean he can't be a trouble-making son of a bitch. And that sure as hell fits the description of whoever—or *whatever*—killed Dave Wolverton."

"So you're thinking demon."

"For starters."

"I'll start running a search for the most common first-order witnesses currently in circulation." Sam glanced at the speedometer and saw they were going eighty. "And you might want to ease up on the gas," he added. "I don't want to end up meeting the local sheriff under the wrong circumstances."

"Yeah, what's his name again?"

"Says here..." Sam checked the notes he'd copied from the internet. "Jack Daniels."

Dean did a double-take.

"No way."

"Would I make something like that up?"

"Sure you would." He glanced at his brother, and then turned his attention back to the road. "I can't wait to meet him." But he slowed the Impala down closer to the speed limit.

"I'm sure the feeling's mutual."

Passing through downtown, Dean swung up to the curb in front of the sheriff's office, parking next to the cruiser. The police vehicle gleamed as if it was newly washed and waxed, its windows down so Sam could hear the radio crackling faintly from inside. As they got out, he noticed an empty sandwich wrapper on the seat.

"Any guesses?" Sam asked.

"Lemmee see. I'm gonna say..." Dean paused, eyes half-closed, as if consulting some inner oracle, "mid-fifties, bald, big belly held in check with a Sam Browne belt."

"Sixties," Sam said, "handlebar moustache, full head of hair that he gets trimmed every Saturday morning over at Babe's Barbershop. Oh yeah, and he's rail-thin—one of those guys who can eat chicken-fried steak three times a day and not gain a pound."

"'Nam vet. Buford Pussar type. From *Walking Tall*."

"*Deliverance* refugee. Civic citations all over his desk."

"Son lost a leg in Desert Storm. Secretly he envies the kid."

"Cheats on his taxes," Sam said, swinging open the door. "Dotes on his wife."

Dean snorted as they entered the sheriff's station.

"Wears women's underwear. Crotchless. The kind that—"

"Is there something I can help you with?"

Both Winchesters froze, and looked round at the same time. Sam was the first to regain his composure.

"We're... ah, looking for the sheriff. Jack Daniels."

The woman in the snugly fitting brown uniform nodded.

"I'm Jacqueline Daniels." She took three steps toward them, the heels of her leather boots clicking smartly on the tiled entryway. She wasn't quite as young as the two women they'd spotted in the street—Sam guessed she was in her early thirties—but her brown eyes and full lips suggested a vitality that wasn't going to fade anytime soon.

Dean, meanwhile, wasn't looking at her eyes at all. He was staring at the badge she wore, which shone as if polished with the same fervor as the cruiser outside.

"Sheriff Daniels, is it?" With some effort, he shifted his attention. "I'm Agent Townes," he said, pulling out his ID, "and this is Agent Van Zandt—"

"Townes?" the sheriff said. "Van Zandt? Is that supposed to be some kind of joke?"

Sam cocked an eyebrow.

"Beg your pardon?"

She shot them a look.

"Your names," she said.

"Look, are you suggesting..." Dean puffed.

"Either you're pulling my leg," she continued, staring at them doubtfully, "Or your superior has one warped sense of humor."

Dean sighed.

"Yeah, and people probably call you Jackie, right?"

"They call me Sheriff Daniels," she responded flatly. The phone started ringing, and she glanced back inside at her desk—which from this distance at least looked as clean and organized as her car. The only exception was a metal ashtray full of what looked like wadded-up bubble gum wrappers.

"Look, can you excuse me a moment? My secretary called in sick today, and I'm a little busy here."

"Sure, take your time." Dean waited while she walked back to pick up the phone, and Sam didn't have to look at his brother to know where his eyes were going. "Hey. What do you think she—" Dean began.

"Stop," Sam said. "Just stop."

"I'm just saying, man, they write songs about this stuff."

"They write songs about going to jail, too," Sam said. "Let's try to avoid doing that in the first ten minutes we're here, okay?"

Sheriff Daniels finished her phone call.

"All right," she said, staying on the far side of her desk, "let's get to it.

"I'm going to be straight with you two," she continued

before either of them could speak. "In case you hadn't noticed, I'm in the middle of a situation, and if I don't come up with some answers, something's going to hit the fan." The phone was ringing again, but the sheriff made no move to answer it, "So if there's something you need from me, make it fast."

"By all means," Sam said.

She gave them another look.

"Well?"

"Let's start with this guy Dave Wolverton, the..." Dean gestured vaguely, "what do you call them? Dress-up guys?"

"They're called re-enactors," the sheriff said. "If you call them dress-up guys, they'll probably clean your clock for you."

"Right. Sorry. *Re-enactors.* According to the report, Wolverton was playing the part of an actual Civil War soldier named Jubal Beauchamp, right? And he shot another dr... re-enactor on the field with a replica of a rifle?"

Daniels nodded curtly.

"A customized model of the classic Springfield musket, built to fire blanks."

"How do you know it wasn't real?"

"I know a replica when I see one." She pointed at a chair off to the right. There was a rifle propped against it. "Like that one."

"May I?" Sam asked.

"Go ahead."

He picked up the replica and hefted it in his hands.

"Feels pretty real to me."

"Of course it feels real," the sheriff said. "It's an ounce-for-ounce recreation of the actual weapon. These re-enactors are intensely devoted to authenticity in every detail. They're hardcore."

"Yeah, so we hear," Sam replied. "What happened to the actual bayonet and gun that Wolverton used on the battlefield?"

"They're in the lab now. Getting tested."

"Okay," Dean said. "So maybe he just got a little carried away and decided the war was still going on? You know, maybe he was a little, I don't know, unbalanced?"

Daniels sighed.

"Maybe you didn't hear what I'm telling you. We're talking about tax attorneys and IT guys who voluntarily choose to dress up in itchy wool uniforms and hobnail boots and do twenty-mile marches in ninety-degree heat. For fun. This is their idea of a good time.

"They're not 'a little unbalanced,'" she continued. "They're certifiable. *But they're all carrying replica guns.* I don't care if you think you're the ghost of Lee Harvey Oswald—you're not killing somebody with a gun that only shoots blanks."

"So you're saying..." Dean started, but then he stopped, not knowing where he was headed.

"So I'm saying that, barring the existence of a wormhole in the time-space continuum which suddenly switched these replicas with real guns and live ammunition, there's no way a weapon like the one Dave Wolverton was carrying yesterday could have possibly done anything like this."

She opened a drawer in her desk, took out a manila folder

and dropped it on the desk, glossy eight-by-tens falling out. Sam picked up the crime-scene photos of a corpse in a Union soldier's uniform.

He passed the first print to Dean. Most of the head had been scalloped away just above the neck and was sprayed out around it. In full color, it looked as though somebody had spilled a particularly messy Italian meal across the grass.

The next photo was a close-up of another re-enactor with one eye gouged out, blood dried over the skin like a theatrical half-mask.

"Wolverton stabbed him with a bayonet," Daniels said, nodding at the side table to the left of the desk. "Just like that one."

Dean picked it up, turning it over in his hands, and tested the edge of the blade against his palm.

"You couldn't cut Wonder Bread with this."

"Gee, you think?" Daniels' eyes, very green and sharp, flicked back and forth between them. Reaching into her desk, she pulled out a piece of gum, unwrapped it, and popped it in her mouth, then wadded up the wrapper and stuffed it in the ashtray.

"Look," she said, "I know you two aren't from around here. So here's what I suggest. Go to the Historical Society, look at some old pictures, check out the battlefield, talk to some re-enactors—"

"We already did that," Dean said.

"Good for you." She took the gum out of her mouth, gave it a look as if it had somehow personally betrayed her, and wadded it up. Into the ashtray it went. "So we're clear, then. Do your own homework, and let me get back to my job. If you come up with any *intelligent* questions, get back to me, okay?"

With that she turned her attention to the paperwork on her desk. Clearly the discussion was over.

"Right," Dean said. "Intelligent questions."

Sam glanced up.

"I've got one."

The sheriff looked up, gazing at him from the depths of bottomless indifference.

"Yes?"

"Wolverton stabbed himself to death with his own bayonet, right?"

"Yes."

"So," he pointed, "what are these marks around his neck?"

"Where?"

"Right here." Sam tapped the photo, indicating Wolverton's throat, where a pair of red friction-burns ringed the flesh. "Like bruises, see?"

"You'd have to ask the coroner."

"You didn't notice anything strange yourself?"

"Anything *strange*?" The sheriff arched one eyebrow. "Are you joking?" But Dean noticed that she didn't actually answer the question.

"Maybe we should talk to the coroner ourselves," he said.

"Be my guest. His office is two blocks away." She glanced at her watch. "Tell you what—it's getting late, but I'll give him a call and let him know you're coming."

"Bruises." Dean was still scrutinizing the photo. "Almost looks like he was choked or something. Right, Sam?"

When there was no immediate answer, he turned to look over his shoulder at his brother, expecting agreement, or at least a nod of acknowledgment.

"Sam?"

But Sam Winchester had done a very strange thing.

He had fallen utterly silent.

SIX

"Okay," Dean said as they walked down the sidewalk toward the coroner's office. "You want to tell me what that was all about?"

"I don't know."

"Really."

"I saw those marks around Wolverton's neck, and I think... it triggered something in my mind." Sam stopped and looked at Dean. "From that dream I had. But I don't remember what it was."

"You're not holding back on me, Sammy, are you?"

Sam shook his head.

"Cuz you know, that never works out."

"I know," Sam said. "I just... it's like whatever happened got erased."

"Well, maybe a look at the corpse will help jog your memory."

* * *

The Mission's Ridge County Coroner's office wasn't much more than a steel doorway in the back of a long brown municipal building just off of Main Street.

Dean and Sam walked past a dumpster and a single vehicle that was parked there, a beige nondescript sedan with government plates. The ground alongside the building was littered with old lottery tickets and cigarette butts, as if someone had spent a long time watching his luck run out.

Dean tried the door.

"Locked." He pressed the buzzer, waited a few seconds, and then started knocking on the wire-reinforced window. "Lights are off. Didn't Sheriff Hottie say she was calling ahead?"

"Maybe the coroner's gone home for the day," Sam offered.

"Or maybe nobody wants to talk to a couple of Yankee boys asking tough questions." Dean stepped back, evaluating the security keypad. "I've gotta say, I'm not feeling a whole lot of Southern hospitality here, Sammy."

"And you're the one who said, 'I *love* the South.'" Sam glanced back in the direction they'd come. "What about the Historical Society?"

"What about it?"

"Maybe we should check that out before it gets any later."

Dean frowned at him.

"You don't want to see the body?"

"Door's locked, Dean."

"So was the vault at the Bellagio, but that didn't stop Ocean's Eleven."

Sam gave him a look.

"I'm just trying to make the most of the time we have."

"So you're not scared of looking at those marks on Wolverton's neck?"

"*Scared*?"

"Yeah, as in, nightmare?" Dean peered at him expectantly.

"I told you, I don't remember."

"And you don't want to."

"Hey, look," Sam said, "if you want me to stay—"

Dean shrugged.

"Nope, you're right," he said. "You go ahead and see what you can dig up. Divide and conquer. Apocalypse freakin' now."

But Sam stood his ground.

"What's this about, Dean?" he demanded. "Is it about you not trusting me? Because if it is, there's not a whole lot of places we can go from there."

"Yeah, you're my brother," Dean said. "But you're also Lucifer's prom dress, and if he's seeding your dreams with hints about the master plan, then *maybe* it *might* be a good idea for you to look at 'em as close as possible. That's all I'm saying."

"What I'm feeling aren't hints, Dean," Sam said, trying to explain as best he could. "They're not clues—if anything, they're *preventing* me from figuring this out. It's more like getting jabbed in the brain with a cattle prod. So forgive me if I don't go actively seeking it out."

"Okay." Dean took out his cell phone. "I'll try the sheriff again, see if I can get her to come over and let me in herself. You do your historical thing, and we'll hook up later and talk it out."

Sam nodded, and left.

Dean stood by the door, watching his brother stride around the corner. There was no mistaking the swiftness of Sam's gait. Whatever the nightmare had left in his mind, Dean knew Sam wasn't ready to deal with it—not directly, anyway.

And when he was, Dean hoped it wouldn't be too late.

Glancing at the wire-reinforced window in the door in front of him, he put away the cell phone and picked up a brick.

"George Clooney was a wuss," he said, and raised the brick. He was about to swing it forward when the lock clicked and the door swung open.

Castiel blinked out at him.

"How long have you been in there?" Dean asked, quickly stepping inside. The coolness of the air conditioning was a relief from the stifling heat outside.

"I just arrived."

"Hey!" a voice cut in. "Who the hell are *you*?"

Dean looked past Castiel, into the office, at an unshaven, thirty-something man in a white Oxford, sleeves rolled up to the elbows, tie tugged down. He'd been in the process of lighting a cigarette, which now dangled from his lower lip in surprise.

"Door was open," Dean said.

"No, it wasn't."

"Are you the coroner?"

"Who's asking?"

Dean badged him.

"Agent Van Zandt, FBI. This is Agent... Zevon." Before Castiel could react, he continued, "Sheriff Daniels gave us the access number in case you were busy."

The coroner regarded Dean and Castiel for a long beat, and the open door behind them, then brought his lighter to the cigarette and put a flame to its tip.

"My name's Todd Winston. And yeah, I'm the coroner." He inhaled and blew a stream of smoke from the corner of his mouth. "But Sheriff Daniels didn't give you the combination to get in. She's not a big fan of the Feds."

"Well, gee golly gosh, Cletus, that just about burns me all up inside," Dean said. "How about we stop worrying about the sheriff and you show me the dead body you got in there."

Grumbling under his breath, Winston led them through the loading area and down the hall to a small office where he ducked inside. When Dean turned to look in after him, he saw that the walls of the office were packed floor to ceiling with books, most of them hardcovers still in their dustjackets.

Emerging again, Winston held a set of keys. He led them around the corner to another, even narrower hallway. A second doorway took them into a storage chamber illuminated from above with long glass florescent tubes that cast a cold declarative light over everything. While the rest of the building had been comfortably cool, here it was downright cold, and Dean was actually glad to be wearing a suit.

In the center of the room stood a steel table with a drain at the bottom, surrounded by cases of sterilized instruments and canisters of fluid and supplies. A bottle of drinking water sat off to one side, half-empty.

Dean paused, the old familiar smells of disinfectant and chemical preservatives pricking his nose. He waited while Winston put on a pair of latex gloves and a lab coat, then turned his attention to the far wall to take hold of a handle.

The coroner twisted the knob, braced himself and pulled out a seven-foot-long drawer, lifting the stainless steel flat-plate to reveal the bin itself.

"This your boy?" Winston asked.

Dean looked down. Pale and naked and somehow flattened, the corpse of Dave Wolverton looked even scrawnier and more pathetic than he'd anticipated. Despite his best efforts to dress and act like a Civil War soldier, it had, ironically, taken nakedness and stillness to complete the transformation. The stab wound on the underside of his chin had been cleaned and sutured, and the coroner's traditional Y-incision was fresh enough that the flesh was still raw and pink where the shears had cut open Wolverton's thoracic cavity.

Small divots of black hair tufted the young man's skinny breastbone and the almost emaciated concavity of his belly. Here was a body that could very easily have come from an actual surgeon's tent back in 1864.

Looks like he died hungry, Dean reflected, the randomness

of the thought surprising him.

He found himself staring at Wolverton's face, the sunken cheekbones and sagging lips. Even vacant and slack, the face had a strange leering quality that put him on edge. He realized that he didn't want to spend any more time with the corpse than he absolutely had to.

"You find anything unusual in the autopsy?" Dean asked.

"Not really," Winston said.

"Toxicology report?"

"Not back yet." He took another drag on his cigarette, then looked around for an ashtray. A used coffee cup fit the bill.

"You don't do that yourself?" Dean asked.

Winston shook his head.

"Lab at the M.E.'s office takes care of that part, down in Waldrop City. Don't have the equipment here."

"Well, I guess that's something to put on your Christmas list, isn't it?" Dean bent down closer to examine the flesh around Wolverton's neck, inspecting the bruises that Sam had first noticed in the photo. "What about these?"

"Twisting abrasions. Rope burns."

"Where'd they come from?"

"Rope," Winston replied, without a hint of humor. "Maybe some kind of cord."

"Thanks," Dean said. "That clears that up."

Winston didn't seem to notice the sarcasm.

"There wasn't anything wrapped around his neck when the sheriff brought the body in. No trace of fibers in the skin either. And you'd see those."

"There are other ways of binding men's souls," Castiel said, leaning forward to touch the hematomas on either side of Wolverton's neck. "Some forms of demonic bondage are not so easily detected."

"Bondage?" Winston glanced at Dean. "What the hell's he talking about?"

Castiel opened his mouth to answer, but Dean cut him off.

"Forget it," Dean said. "Is there an inventory of what Wolverton had with him when he died?"

"Sheriff's office is still typing it up." He glanced at the doorway. "I just remembered, I gotta make a phone call."

Without awaiting a response, he walked out, leaving Dean and Castiel alone with the corpse.

"Well, might as well give this a shot," Dean said, glancing at his companion and reaching into his back pocket. He pulled out an index card and began reading the *Rituale Romanum*.

"*Deus, et Pater Domini nostri Jesu Christi, invoco nomen sanctum tuum...*"

"You don't have it memorized by now?" Castiel asked, completely in earnest.

"I got sick of everybody correcting me all the time so I just wrote it down," Dean said, and then he kept reading. "*...et celmentiam tuam supplex exposco...*"

Without warning Wolverton's corpse jerked a little in the bin, hard enough that one hand twitched and fell palm-open, and the fingers quivered and twitched.

The corpse's head rolled slightly to one side.

"*...ut adversus hunc, et omnem immundum spiritum...*"

"Something's happening," Castiel said.

Dean paused and glanced down.

Something black was emerging from Wolverton's left ear. At first he thought it was some kind of fluid, and then he realized that it was alive. Tiny, cilia-like legs—dozens of them—wiggled around it. With weird, deliberate speed, the black thing began to scurry like a malformed cockroach across Wolverton's pale cheek, as if making its way toward his eyes.

As Dean stared at it it stopped, frozen in place.

It's looking at me.

The hairs rose up on the back of his neck.

That's impossible, it doesn't even have—

Then, with a high-pitched shriek, the black thing sprang upward, launching itself at Dean's face.

He jerked backward on reflex and the thing hit the floor. He lunged and stomped on it, crushing it under his heel, then grimaced at the sticky stuff that spattered outward from the bottom of his shoe. The thing was still wiggling, pulsing furiously as it crawled upward, onto his ankle.

He could feel it sucking against his skin, pulling as it slithered upward toward his calf.

"It's still moving!" Dean shouted. *"Get it off!"*

Without hesitating, Castiel picked up the bottled water. He closed his eyes, murmuring over it briefly, then dumped the water over Dean's lower leg.

There was a smoking hiss and the thing gave another shriek. Dean felt it go limp against his skin. He yanked up his soaking wet pant-leg and saw nothing but a faint reddish mark just above his Achilles tendon.

Grabbing a piece of paper towel, he wiped the last of the holy water from his leg, wadded up the wet towel and tossed it in the trash.

"What *was* that?" he asked, trying to calm his own breathing.

"Moa'ah," Castiel said.

"What?"

"A kind of demonic afterbirth unique to this region of the American South." The angel scowled. "I have not seen its like since the Civil War battlegrounds. When angels and demons skirmished over the souls of the dead."

"And now it's back," Dean said, peering with disgust at the bottom of his shoe. "But why? And why Wolverton?"

Castiel looked at him.

"He was touched by the Witness."

"So your Witness used this guy as some kind of demonic snot-rag?"

"You don't understand," Castiel told him. "Moa'ah is a footnote in the Luciferian apotheca—one of its most obscure calling cards. It shouldn't exist anymore. Its very presence here is a harbinger of the Apocalypse. And the Witness knows this. He wants us to know it."

"And you're looking for this guy?" Dean asked. "On purpose?"

"I need to find him."

"Yeah, well," Dean shook his head, "good luck with that."

* * *

They found Winston back in his office, phone to his ear. Dean walked over and hit the 'disconnect' button.

"Hey!" the coroner snapped, leaping to his feet. For a second it seemed as if he might take a step closer, but then he saw something in Dean's face that stopped him in his tracks.

"Who else was alone with that body?" Dean demanded.

"What?"

"You heard me. Besides yourself, who's been back there?"

"Nobody. Sheriff Daniels, I guess. That's about it. Whole thing happened right there on the battlefield, in front of God and everybody. If there was a rope around Wolverton's neck, somebody would have seen it." Winston sounded a little desperate now. "Right?"

"The rope is the least of your worries," Dean said, glancing up at the ceiling. "You have surveillance cameras here? Motion detectors?"

Castiel looked at Dean.

"The Witness has full demonic powers. It could have passed through here entirely unnoticed."

Winston's eyes widened.

"*What?*"

"Bull. Anything that skeevy's gonna leave a trace."

Castiel shook his head.

"But—"

Dean cut in, turning back to the coroner.

"When does the toxicology report get back?" he asked.

Winston swallowed hard.

"Tomorrow, probably."

"Did you find anything else out of the ordinary, inside the body or on his clothes? Any kind of markings or ritualistic burns and scars?"

"No." But there was something in his voice.

"You're sure?"

"Yes." Winston stared helplessly down at the desk top. "Jesus, yes!"

Dean's eyes flicked to the phone.

"Let's see who you decided to reach out and touch," he muttered, clicking 'speaker' and hitting the redial button.

"Don't do that," Winston pleaded. "You really don't want to—"

"Oh, but I do," Dean replied while the phone rang, and finally picked up. A woman's voice came through the speaker.

"Hello," she said. "It's—"

Dean frowned at Castiel.

"Wait, I *know* that voice." He glared back down at the phone. "Who is this?"

But the recorded voice on the phone had already continued talking.

"—Candy. Me and my friends are having a party in the jacuzzi but we lost our bikini tops, and now..." The voice began to sigh and breathe more heavily. "You just *have* to help us find them. Just enter a credit card number for three minutes of—"

"You know this woman?" Castiel asked.

Dean cut the call off mid-sentence and looked at Winston. The coroner's face was blazing red now.

"The township better not have been paying for that call," Dean muttered, turning to leave. "And we'll be back to take a look at that toxicology report."

"Sure," Winston said. "Whatever. Just... how about a little warning next time, huh?"

"He was not lying," Castiel said as they stepped outside into the gathering dark.

"I know," Dean sighed. "Which leaves us with exactly bupkes."

"Not necessarily." They walked down the sidewalk beneath the streetlights. "Wolverton could have encountered the Witness on the battlefield, or—"

"Hold on." Dean stopped walking. "You've been talking a lot about the Witness this and the Witness that. But if this Witness hung out with Jesus and it's got a thing for nooses, that leaves me with about one guess."

"And that is?"

"Judas. You're hunting Judas."

Castiel shook his head.

"I don't know," he said.

"Why not?"

"Judas was more concerned with temptation and betrayal than with bloody violence."

"Yeah, well, if there's one thing I know about humanity, it's that betrayal can get pretty messy when there's gunfire involved."

Up ahead, Dean heard boisterous voices and laughter. He

turned around, taking notice of their surroundings for the first time. They had stopped walking a block away from a massive old church, its planks looking as if they had survived centuries of warfare and harsh weather, like a shipwrecked battleship that had come to rest here.

Crowds of people in suits and dresses were pouring out of its high arched doorway.

"Is this a…?" Castiel asked.

"A wedding." There was a burst of applause and cheers, and Dean watched as the bride and groom came down the church steps, heading in the direction of a limousine that was waiting at the curb.

She was wearing an antique wedding dress; he wore a Confederate soldier's uniform so authentic that Dean could actually see clouds of dust rising from its shoulders.

"You're kidding. They get *married* in this stuff?"

"Love is a battlefield," Castiel said.

Dean stared at him.

"What?"

"It's a song I heard recently."

Dean barely suppressed a smile and turned away from the angel.

"You're something, Cass, you know that?" There was no response, and Dean paused without turning. "You just disappeared on me, didn't you?"

Sure enough, when he looked back, Castiel was indeed gone.

SEVEN

Sam arrived at the pillared façade of the Mission's Ridge Historical Society, having stopped by the Impala to discard his FBI jacket and tie. He climbed the granite steps to the front door, a slab of oak with an imposing iron handle, fully expecting to find it locked. Instead, it swung open on well-oiled hinges.

With a sense of coolness spreading over him, he stepped inside.

The entryway was windowless, darker than he'd expected, and the scrape of his feet echoed with a stony acoustic resonance that came from old places that had been left alone for long periods of time. He could smell camphor and old paper, canvas and mildew, and his eyes were still struggling to adjust.

For a moment he wasn't even sure how big the entryway was.

"Help you?" a man's voice asked behind him.

"That depends." Sam turned, and a flashlight beam passed over his face, momentarily blinding him. "You work here?"

"I do," the man said. "Sorry about the flashlight. Wiring troubles. She's a lovely old building, but the electrical system can be a royal bitch, if you'll excuse my French." The man reached over to a fuse box embedded in the wall and fiddled with something inside for a moment. There was a loud *clank*, and lights came shuddering on.

"Ah, there we go."

Looking up, Sam saw they were standing in a wide foyer. In front of him stood a man wearing an Atlanta Braves baseball cap, black t-shirt and faded Levis. He didn't look much past his mid-thirties, but the first wrinkles of middle age had already settled around the corners of his eyes and mouth, giving his face a comfortable, lived-in look. The stubble on his jaw was a salt-and-pepper mix that gleamed a little in the light.

Next to him stood a young boy of perhaps eleven or twelve, also wearing jeans and a t-shirt—blond, fair-skinned, with wide, curious blue eyes that seemed to be taking in everything at once. The man held a huge, ancient toolbox, and the boy stood in unconscious imitation of the man's pose, cradling a stack of thick hardcover books under one arm. There was no question that they were father and son.

"I'm Tommy McClane," the man said, putting the tools down and wiping his right hand on his jeans before extending it to Sam. "This is my boy Nate."

"Pleased to meet you," the boy said formally.

Sam shook their hands, smiling faintly at the gravity with which the boy shuffled his load of books around so that he could offer his own small palm.

"You work for the Historical Society?" Sam asked.

"We *are* the Historical Society," Tommy said wryly. "Old Pop Meechum used to run the place, but since his stroke laid him out, it's just been me and Nate taking care of things." He squinted a little. "You got a name, or should I just call you the Phantom Stranger?"

Sam smiled again.

"I'm Sam."

"Sam it is." Tommy McClane glanced down at his son. "Nate, why don't you go put those in the library, see if there's anything else we need to pick up in there. Meet us back in the museum."

"Yessir."

Tommy watched him go, then nodded back in the other direction.

"Come on back, why don't you." Picking up the toolbox, he sauntered down the corridor, then stopped again as something occurred to him. "You're not from around here, I'm guessing."

"No."

"So are you in town for this whole re-enactment bugaboo out by the creek?"

"You might say that."

"Bunch of crazy rednecks running around the woods with toy guns, acting the fool," he said, watching for Sam's reaction.

"Am I right?"

"Actually," Sam said, "I think it's pretty impressive, their commitment to authenticity. They're like living historians."

Tommy squinted at him a moment, then grinned.

"You're all right, you know that."

"Excuse me?"

"Y'see, you're talking to one of those fools right now." Tommy held up a hand, showing Sam a tarnished ring. "Confederate States of America. My great-grandfather wore this ring out on that very battlefield. Not that I support everything the South was fighting for, mind you. There wasn't anybody happier than me to see an African-American in the White House. About damn time, I say. Nate and I drove up to DC for his Inauguration.

"But I'm still proud as hell of those men that laid down their lives in the line of duty, just the same." He turned again and continued down the corridor.

Sam nodded and followed him, not entirely sure what to make of this man and his peculiar mix of backwoods erudition and self-effacement. Whatever the case, though, he'd already decided that he liked Tommy McClane. And at the moment he wasn't exactly in the position to be picky about his allies.

"Well, listen," Tommy said, opening a closet and putting his toolbox away, "I been running my gums a mile a minute, so tell me—what can I do for you?"

"I was hoping you could tell me about a Confederate soldier named Jubal Beauchamp."

"Beauchamp?" Tommy glanced up, making no effort to hide his surprise. "What do you want to know about *him* for?"

"Well, I'm sure you heard about what happened yesterday with Dave Wolverton. He was playing the role of Beauchamp. I want to know if you have any information about him. The original soldier, I mean."

Tommy peered at him for a long time, his expression impossible to read. He cocked his head slightly to one side.

"You're not a cop, are you?"

"No."

"Federal Agent?"

Sam took in a breath, meeting Tommy's deep gray eyes. He knew this was probably his last chance to lie. Going on instinct, he shook his head.

"No."

"Didn't think so. So what's your interest?"

"I..." Sam started, and realized he'd left himself without any options. "Let's just say that what happened on that battlefield yesterday doesn't have a reasonable explanation. And those are the kind of events that tend to get my attention."

Tommy stared at him again for a moment, then burst out laughing.

"You're a *hunter*," he said, and slapped Sam on the shoulder. "Now it all makes sense."

Sam stepped back, stunned.

"I've never heard your name before," he said. "I haven't heard about anyone working in this area."

"I was expecting Rufus," McClane said. "What happened to him?"

"Something came up. My brother and I stepped in." Sam shook his head, still processing the information that the other man had given him. "So you've hunted with Rufus Turner?"

"Not actively. Hunting's not exactly a life you want to share with a young kid, if you know what I mean."

Sam nodded.

"I do."

"Nate's mom died four years ago. Car accident, couple of teenagers out on a first date, everybody stone-cold sober— just about as accidental as those things can be. Nobody to blame and no survivors. It was hard on both of us, especially the boy. Getting through it, I realized how important it was to be around for him." McClane shook his head. "Doesn't mean I can't keep my eyes and ears open, though, give a shout out to the hunters when things start looking nasty."

"Is it nasty here?"

McClane gave a dark nod.

"See for yourself."

Tommy led Sam through a warren of tidy, interconnected rooms, deeper into the building. Walking past rows of glass display cases, Sam caught glimpses of old pistols and muskets, yellowed documents, boots and uniforms, all carefully mounted and labeled beneath the track lighting. Every time he thought he'd reached Tommy, the man had moved on to the next exhibit.

Turning another corner, he finally caught up with him.

Tommy had stopped in front of a display showing the first, second, and third National Flags of the wartime South.

"What kind of activity have you noticed around the town?" he asked the historian. "Was there anything unusual before the incident?"

"For starters?" McClane said. "Place is crawling with ghosts."

"Metaphorically?"

McClane gave him a look.

"Do I look like the kind of guy who would say that metaphorically?"

"I just meant—"

"You see those train tracks running through town? Once upon a time the Confederacy had a train running right through Main Street and out to the battlefield. Had themselves a flatcar with a Gatling gun mounted on it, blasted the first wave of Union soldiers all to hell." He nodded. "Train's tucked away in the railway shed, but the tracks are still there. You listen at night, folks say you can still hear the whistle crying out."

Sam cocked an eyebrow.

"Really."

"There's plenty more." Tommy stopped and pointed around the corner. "Right through here."

Sam followed him into a room and saw Nate waiting for them there. The library was a bright place with high ceilings and wooden bookcases lining the walls, a stepladder on rails, stretching up to the top. Oak reading tables and individual study carrels gleamed under rows of swan-necked lamps. Off to the left sat another desk full of neatly arranged computer equipment and a monitor. He saw several framed diplomas and certificates hanging on the wall.

"This is impressive," Sam said. "Does the town pay for all this?"

"Folks around here take their history seriously," Tommy said. And then, with a slight note of pride, "Me and Nate did a lot of the carpentry ourselves." He reached out and tousled Nate's hair. "Do me a favor, son, and pull down those folios up in the far right corner there, see 'em? May 1863. Letters A to C."

The boy nodded and scurried up the ladder, gathering a stack of volumes that looked as if they'd been bound in animal-hide and hauling them over to the table. Tommy lifted the cover and flipped through stiff pages so old that they crackled as he turned them.

"Jubal Beauchamp was a son of a bitch," Tommy began. "Excuse me for saying so, but there's no other word for it. He came up from Hattiesburg, about twenty miles from here, the only son of a Tennessee preacher who'd moved here on account of some kind of hijinks with his flock. Don't know the particulars, but I can guess 'em well enough, I suppose.

"Anyhow, Jubal was being groomed for the pulpit like his daddy, but just after seminary school, something happened to him that changed his way of looking at things."

"You seem to know a lot about him," Sam said.

"Let's just say you aren't the first hunter to come around asking about him. Dollar for dollar, it doesn't get much spookier than Beauchamp. Lookit."

Tommy pointed down at a smaller leather-bound diary that appeared to have been stitched directly into the spine of the larger volume.

"See this?" he asked. "Beauchamp's private journal. Bought it off a collector in Louisiana back in '05." Tommy opened it, and the smell that came out was even more like dead animal skin with a tincture of something more feral and pungent.

His tone became reverent.

"Want to see something *really* scary?"

Sam bent down to examine the lines of tight, neat handwriting that crawled over the pages. It was full of Scripture—lines that appeared to have been copied directly from the Bible, and what he could make out in between seemed almost mundane. There were notes Beauchamp had made to himself, lists of books and annotations of sermons and lectures.

"Now," Tommy pointed, "look at this. May 1862. He leaves the seminary and joins up with the Confederate army."

"The pages are blank," Sam said.

"Only a couple of them." Tommy turned further into the diary. "Here's where it gets good."

The difference was unmistakable. Beauchamp's neat, tidy penmanship had become a shaky, almost violent scrawl, as if written while he was on horseback, or under the influence of some profoundly deranging psychotropic cocktail. Mixed in between were drawings, pentagrams and demonic insignias, that covered almost the entire page.

> *Almighty one, Lord of the Flies, Immortal Black Father, keeper of goats, receive my offering and bestow upon me the full mantle of thy wrath. Thine is the kingdom and the power to come, forever and ever.*

Sam blinked, and looked up at his host.

"It's a desecration of the Lord's Prayer."

McClane stared at him.

"How do you know that?"

"These words here, they..." Sam began, and then he stopped. Looking down at the page, he realized that the text he'd been reading was written not only in an entirely different language, but in letters that didn't remotely resemble the Roman alphabet.

Yet to his eyes they had automatically translated themselves.

Sam blinked again, feeling his pulse beating harder in his throat, until he could hear the blood thumping in his ears. Closing his eyes and opening them again, he looked down at the letters on the page and saw only an impenetrable forest of symbols.

"I don't..." he managed, "I don't even know how I read that. I don't even know what language that is."

"It's Coptic," McClane said, his voice sounding hollow with surprise. "It's an extinct Egyptian language. *Nobody* speaks it—not anymore."

"Well..." Sam swallowed, getting his bearings, "things have been a little different for me lately."

"Sounds like it," Tommy said warily. He regarded Sam silently for a moment, then seemed to come to a decision. "And speaking of different, check this out." He dug deeper into the diary and pulled out a thick, stiff square of daguerreotype, holding it by the edges as he passed it to Sam. "This is the only known photograph of old Jubal."

Sam looked at it. The photo showed a gaunt, hatchet-faced soldier in a dirty, ill-fitting uniform. His eyes were lost in the shadow of the slouch cap, though there was no mistaking the dark grin that had twisted its way across his face. Beauchamp looked like a man with a secret locked in his heart—one so black and eager with promise that, once released, there would be no stopping it.

Around his neck, he wore an old rope tied into a noose.

"Do you have a magnifying glass?" Sam asked, and then he glanced back at the computer. "Or better yet, a scanner. I need to see this close up."

"Sure," Nate piped up, and then he glanced up at his father. "Can I, Dad?"

"You know how to use it," Tommy said, and the boy ran off with the old photograph, headed over to one of the computers that Sam had seen on his way into the library.

Once Nate was out of earshot, McClane bent closer to Sam.

"Listen," he said. "There're some more entries in that journal, stuff I haven't been able to translate. Considering what you just did with that Coptic writing, maybe you want to take a look at it? See if you can make heads or tails of it."

Sam flipped the next page of Beauchamp's diary. By now the handwriting was so different that it had to have come from a different person entirely. The letters were twisted and sharp, freely intermingled with symbols and characters along the page, and yet—

Sam stared, he saw the lines transforming themselves, swimming a little across the stained pages, the letters themselves becoming somehow familiar.

"Someone else wrote this part," he explained. "It says that Jubal Beauchamp was killed and brought back to life... through the powers of the noose..." He paused, wanting to get it right. "The man who did it was a Civil War doctor named Percy. When the doctor finished experimenting on him, he buried Beauchamp's remains in an iron coffin, his spirit held fast by a spell from which it could not escape."

When he looked up, Tommy was staring at him.

"You're not just an ordinary hunter, are you?" the man asked.

"I—" Sam considered a variety of answers, then just shook his head. "No."

"Didn't think so."

There was a long silence between them, not quite awkward, but not comfortable either. Finally Sam spoke.

"I appreciate all your help with this."

Tommy didn't reply right away. Instead he scraped back his chair, turned and nodded around behind him at the doorway where they'd come in. Above it, Sam saw a small dark object not much bigger than a man's hand attached directly to the wall above the entryway. He got up and looked more closely.

It was a bundle of what looked like hair or fur, wrapped carefully around an arrangement of roots and chicken bones.

"Hoodoo protection sigil," Sam said. "Did you make it yourself?"

"I watch out over me and mine," Tommy said evenly. "Don't mistake my meaning. I've been to college. As I said, I'm not some backwoods autodidactic hillbilly. But this is the South. You'd be surprised what we see down here." He considered Sam. "Or maybe you wouldn't."

"Does anybody know where Beauchamp was buried?"

"Nope. Folklore says that he and dozens of other soldiers were buried somewhere in a mass grave out on the battlefield. Unmarked and lost to time. Probably best left that way, if you ask me."

"Thanks for the input," Sam said.

Tommy McClane nodded. Something still seemed to be bothering him, however—a sense of restlessness that he couldn't quite articulate. As Sam turned to go, he spoke in a low voice.

"Sam?"

"Yes?"

"I know you're a hunter, so you know what you're getting yourself into, but this is bloody ground. I hope for your sake that whatever you're doing, you'll step lightly." He took in a breath and let it out. "Some of this stuff isn't buried too deep."

"You know what Faulkner said about the past," Sam said.

"Yeah. He said it's not dead. It ain't even past." And then, brightening a little, Tommy added, "Leave me your phone number and email and I'll have Nate send that scan to you as an attachment."

Sam nodded.

"And hey."

"Yes?"

"You want to hear how the South *really* lost the war?"

Sam frowned.

"I'm not sure I—"

"Come on by the house after dinner, if you want. 440 Baxter Springs Road. We'll sit out on the porch and drink iced tea and talk about spooks. Bring your brother…"

"Dean," Sam said, and he agreed.

The boy returned, putting the photo carefully back in its proper place, then the three of them wove their way back to the front door.

Sam waved goodbye to Tommy and Nate, stepped out into the night and down the front steps, and back through town.

EIGHT

The bar was small, crowded and smoky, with a pool table in the back. The Georgia Satellites were rocking 'Battleship Chains' on the jukebox at a volume just short of thunderous, while a mix of patrons in Civil War garb and modern-day clothing tried to find room to dance.

Behind the counter, a Confederate flag hung next to the mounted head of a buck. Someone long ago had tacked a handwritten sign on a paper plate above the deer's head, proclaiming 'Nice rack.'

"I'm guessing they don't have wi-fi here," Dean muttered across the booth. "I feel like I'm in the *Star Wars* cantina."

Sam opened the laptop and looked over at him.

"Where's Cass?"

Dean shrugged.

"Off on heavenly business, I guess." He took a long drink from the glass in front of him, but the beer seemed to do him little good. "Here's some shocking news. Dave Wolverton wasn't just your typical airport restaurant waiter. I said a little of the exorcism right over his corpse, and stuff got messy in a hurry."

"What happened?" Sam asked.

"Turns out that Cass's Witness has itself a nice little calling card. Something called Moa'ah. Stuff went crawling up my leg. Cass had to burn it off with holy water."

"Moa'ah?" Sam turned to the keyboard. "How do you spell that?"

"Gee, you know, Sammy, I forgot to look at its nametag." Dean sipped his beer. "I'm fine, by the way."

"Sorry. I just—"

"Forget it," Dean said. "We'll call Bobby and see if he's ever heard of it. You find anything out at the Historical Society?"

"Well… if I can just get a signal… yes!" As he accessed his email Sam told his brother about the encounter with Tommy and Nate.

"Sonuvagun," Dean said. "Well, at least your guy wasn't a closet pervert. And it's nice to have some help on this one."

Nodding his agreement, Sam opened the email from Nate, downloaded the attachment, and turned the laptop around so Dean could see the old photo of Jubal Beauchamp.

"Here's our guy," he said. "The *original* guy."

"And let me guess, that noose around his neck…?"

"—isn't just any old noose." Sam tapped a key, magnifying the image and correcting the resolution so the pixels sharpened into focus. Then he pointed. "What are these?"

"Knots?"

"They seem to have a specific arrangement of some sort." Sam clicked on a link, bringing up a new window and an image of an old engraving of a rope twisted into complex interwoven patterns. "Have you ever heard of the Judas noose?" he asked.

Dean smacked the table with his palm.

"I freakin' *knew* it."

"Knew what?"

"Judas," Dean replied, his voice low. "That's *got* to be his Witness."

"Listen to this," Sam said. "According to the lore, if you could recreate the exact combination of knots that Judas used and place the noose over someone's head, you'd release a strong demonic curse. Gives the wearer unholy powers, protects them from death... and eventually drives them mad. In the homicidal sense of the word."

He hesitated.

"And there's something else."

"There always is."

"I'm pretty sure this noose—whatever else it might represent—was part of the nightmare I had."

"So it's already in your head," Dean said. "How do we get rid of it before it does a number on your sanity? It's not like you've got a lot to spare."

"I haven't figured it out yet." Sam lowered the laptop screen enough to meet his brother's gaze. "But I'm guessing from the fact that you're sitting here empty-handed that you didn't find the noose at the coroner's office, either."

"Nope." Dean picked up his glass, where the beer seemed to have disappeared almost against his will. "The coroner's a tool, by the way. More or less useless."

"Yeah, I gathered that," Sam said. "So should we go back to the sheriff?"

Dean waved away the idea.

"Screw her," he said. "She's just as bad as he is."

"No, Dean—" Sam began.

"I mean it," Dean pressed. "I've been thinking about it. Back at her office, she said 'like that one.' That means she didn't have the actual weapons Wolverton used. So where'd *they* go? And why didn't she want to help us, knowing we're Feds?

"They're probably in cahoots together. What's more… "

"Dean, I'm trying to tell you, she's..."

"Hot," Dean said, "sure. Believe me, I wouldn't kick her out of bed for eating crackers. But if you think I'm gonna give her a free pass on account of that—"

"No, I'm trying to say that she's... standing right... behind you."

A look of disgust covered Dean's face. Slowly he turned around and saw Sheriff Daniels standing next to them, not two feet away, where she'd been listening to their entire conversation. She was glaring right at him.

"Were you saying something about Todd Winston?" she asked. "Please, continue."

"Okay." Dean nodded, stubbornly unrepentant. "How about, he's a jerk and a sleaze? Do you even *know* the guy?"

"I ought to," Sheriff Daniels said. "He's my brother-in-law."

"I should've known. Is everybody in this town related?"

"Not only that," she said, "we're all inbred racist hicks. What's your point, Agent Townes?"

"He told me there's no toxicology report available yet. It's been almost twenty-four hours. What's going on with that?"

"This isn't New York or Los Angeles, Mister Federal Agent," she said dryly. "Things move at a more languid pace down here."

"Languid, huh? Good *SAT* word." Dean glanced across the room. A girl who couldn't have been much older than eighteen was slow-dancing with a biker twice her age. He was wearing a Mojo Nixon t-shirt, and both his hands were cupping the swell of her buttocks as she ground against him. "Seems like some of it moves pretty fast."

"I beg your pardon?" she said, turning to look.

"Nothing. Forget it."

"Well, here's a word for you," Sheriff Daniels said turning back and pinning him with another glare. "Judge. As in, 'judge not, lest ye be judged.'" She smiled then, making a completely unconvincing show of hospitality. "Enjoy your stay."

With that, she turned on her heel and left.

Sam and Dean were leaving the bar, on their way to the Impala, when they heard the voice behind them. Turning, they saw a young Rebel soldier step into the streetlight, walking toward them in full uniform, complete with a slouch cap.

The guy couldn't have been on the legal side of twenty-one—he was pale and skinny, his cheekbones high and sharp. As far as lack of nourishment went, he almost looked *too* realistic. A lot like Wolverton's corpse. For a second Dean wondered if he was actually seeing a ghost, the revenant of a dead Confederate soldier.

Then he noticed the gray coat's iPod.

Approaching them, the young man removed the white earbuds. Dean caught a faint buzz of electric guitars before the soldier switched it off and gazed at them with pale blue eyes.

"I saw you two talking to the sheriff back there," he said. "Are you investigating what happened to Dave Wolverton?"

"That's right," Sam said. "You knew him?"

"You could say that."

"Look," Dean cut in, "no offense, Billy Yank, but it's late and we've had a long day. If you can tell us anything that might help..."

"I lived with him," the soldier said. "For almost a year."

"You mean roommates?"

"We were dating."

"You and Wolverton?"

The soldier removed the slouch cap. Dean found himself staring as the hairpins came out, releasing a fluid tumble of brown hair that framed the angular face, immediately changing the subtle geometry of the cheek-bones, eyes and lips. The skinny, somewhat effeminate male soldier in front of him had just transformed into an attractive young brunette.

"Wow," Dean said, not at all sure how he felt about this.

"Okay."

"My name is Sarah Rafferty," the woman said. "Dave and I actually met at the TGI Fridays at the airport where we both worked about a year and a half ago. He's the one that got me into all this."

"That's... cool. I guess?"

"Crazy as it sounds," the woman said, "there's actually an historical precedent. There were some women on both sides who put on uniforms and fought alongside the men, sometimes as drummer boys or powder monkeys, or even infantry. Not many, but a few."

"So you and Dave were together," Sam said. "For how long?"

"A year or so. He started coming into the restaurant talking about all this stuff. After a while I caught the bug. I was actually a communications major, but I minored in American History. Eventually Dave asked me to go to a re-enactment up in Gettysburg, and I was hooked." She smiled a little at the memory. "He liked that it was our secret. Even the other guys in the 32nd didn't know that I was a woman."

"So were you two still involved when he died?" Dean asked.

Sarah shook her head.

"I broke things off a couple of months ago."

"Why?"

"It was Dave—he changed. I mean, for a while I was legitimately impressed, how intensely he focused on nailing every detail with absolute authenticity. But something was just different. He wasn't Dave anymore. He was Jubal Beauchamp all the time. It was like he had disappeared into the persona."

"Uh-huh."

"There were problems at work. With the customers, I mean. We work in an airport restaurant, so we have people from everywhere. Dave would start talking to them about the Confederacy, and how the South should have won the war. It didn't exactly go over well."

"Ouch," Dean said.

"They had to fire him. But Dave didn't care. He said it gave him more time to concentrate on his *real* work."

"Being Jubal Beauchamp?" Sam said.

"That's right."

"Yikes," Dean said. "Single white Confederate."

Sam shot Dean a look, and turned back to Sarah.

"Did you notice any one particular moment when it all changed?"

"Actually," Sarah said, "that's why I'm here. After it ended, I started trying to figure out where it all went wrong.

"Dave and I came to Mission's Ridge about three months ago, for a wedding. One of the guys in the 32nd was getting married at the old Pentecostal Church in town."

"I saw someone else getting married there today," Dean said.

"They do it all the time," Sarah said. "The re-enactors love to use that church because it's the only building in town the Union Army didn't burn down when they marched through Mission's Ridge. Phil Oiler, did you meet him?"

"I think so."

"Insurance salesman from Atlanta. He was the one getting married, and of course he wanted to do it in full uniform. So we all suited up for it, the 32nd Georgia in full parade dress." She paused, her expression darkening. "Except sometime between the ceremony and the reception, Dave and Phil disappeared."

"Disappeared where?"

"That's just it, nobody knew. For almost an hour they were just gone. Of course the bride was furious, because the photographer was out front and everybody was standing around waiting to go to the reception. Then, at the last minute, they showed up again like nothing had happened. People thought they were out getting high.

"But Dave didn't do that." She drew in a breath and let it out slowly. "That night at the reception was the first time I noticed how different he was. He started asking me to call him Jubal. I thought he was drunk, but it just kept happening. His accent got stronger. He started getting rough with me... when we were alone. And the things that came out of his mouth—they were awful. A couple of weeks later, I couldn't take it anymore. I packed up and moved out. Then when I heard what happened yesterday..." Her eyes shone. "I had to come back here."

"In full uniform?" Dean said.

The woman paused, weighing her words carefully.

"I wanted to talk to Phil," she said at last. "I thought maybe he might be able to tell me more about what happened to him and Dave in the church that day. And, of course, I couldn't come to him as Sarah Rafferty. I had to be Private Will Tanner."

"*Did* you talk to Phil?" Sam asked. "Did you ask him about what happened at the wedding?"

She nodded.

"He said that he and Dave just went down to the basement to smoke a joint." Her blue eyes flashed brighter now, flinty with anger. "He was lying to me. And now Dave's dead."

"Did you talk to the sheriff?"

"I tried to. She's not interested. I don't understand. I thought... I guess I thought if I came clean and told her the truth about Dave and me, that she might dig a little deeper and help me figure out what went wrong. But it's like she's on some whole other mission."

"Like what?" Sam asked, his curiosity piqued.

"I don't know. It's like she knows more than she's letting on... like she's after something."

Sam and Dean traded a look, neither of them speaking for a moment. Then Sam turned back to Sarah.

"What exactly did the sheriff say to you?"

"Well, I told her about what happened at the church. She was really interested in that. But when I couldn't answer any of her questions, she just lost interest." Sarah frowned. "Why, do you think she's got something to hide, too?"

"It's too soon to say," Sam said.

"Look," Sarah said. "If you know something, you have to tell me. I cared for Dave. I want to know the truth."

She reached up and rubbed her eyes. "That's why I thought maybe the two of you—I mean, I heard you say that you were Federal Agents, so..."

Sam touched her arm.

"We'll do what we can. In the meantime, if you think of anything else, don't talk to the sheriff. Come directly to us." He handed her a card with his cell phone number on it.

"I will." She glanced down at the slouch cap, still gripped in one hand. "You know my secret now anyway."

"In the morning," Dean said, "we'll go back out to the battlefield and talk to Phil Oiler about his wedding day."

"Thank you both." She held out a slip of paper. "Here's my cell."

"We'll be in touch," Dean said, grabbing the paper. As they walked back to the car, Dean glanced at the number again and exhaled deeply, puffing out his cheeks with a long, exhausted sigh. "What a day. Right now all I want to do is go back to the motel, crack open a nightcap and watch a little Casa Erotica."

Sam shook his head.

"Not tonight, Dean."

"What? *Why?*"

"I've got some people I want you to meet."

NINE

Sam called Bobby on the way out to the McClanes' house, giving Dean directions while he asked Bobby about the Judas noose and the Moa'ah. There was a long pause and he heard pages rattling in the background.

"Looks like the noose is part of Civil War lore from the beginning," Bobby's voice came back. "There're even songs about it."

"What about the Moa'ah?"

"From what I can figure, it sounds like you're talking about two sides of the same coin. Down in that particular region of the South, Moa'ah's the animating force behind every bad kind of mojo you can imagine. Like the fuel that makes it go. Sounds like your dead Civil War soldier must've gotten some on him when he wore the noose."

"So even if the noose itself is gone..." Sam started.

"The Moa'ah sticks around. Yeah."

"So what do we do to stop it?"

"For now, nothing. Just stay the hell out of its way till I get a better handle on the info. I'll call you back as soon as I've got something."

"Thanks, Bobby." Sam cut off the call and turned to Dean. Then he noticed that the Impala had slowed down enough that he could see individual pebbles and blades of grass in the headlights. "What's wrong?"

"We're lost," Dean said. "Gotta be."

"No, we're not." Sam pointed straight ahead through the windshield. "Tommy gave me directions. Take a left here. Look—up on the hill."

"Tommy, huh? Sounds like you two got pretty chummy."

"Well..." Sam said. "When he found out that we were hunters..."

Dean's head swiveled to stare at him.

"Wait a minute," he said, his voice growing louder. "You *told* him? What's the point of having a cover story if you're gonna...?"

"Hold on, it's all right," Sam said, cutting him off. "I didn't tell him—he figured it out himself. He's the one who called Rufus."

"Sure, that's what he *told* you—"

Sam felt himself getting hot under the collar.

"Sorry, Dean, but I didn't have my portable polygraph test on me at the time."

"That's the point—you're not supposed to *need* one," Dean replied, refusing to back down. "Never trust a stranger, Sammy, that's Demon Hunting 101. Suppose this McClane guy was dropping Rufus's name to get to us. Now we're walking in there blind, and he already knows everything about us."

"Not everything," Sam said.

"What, you didn't get around to telling him that you jump-started the Apocalypse? Give it time—he'll figure that out, too."

"Fine, I'll tell you what," Sam replied, "I'll call Bobby back and ask if he knows him. That'll prove he's on the level."

"Forget it," Dean grumbled, "we're already here."

Sam turned and peered through the windshield, into the beams of the headlights. They were curving along a circular drive, and the plantation house spread itself above them, half-lost amid the cottonwoods and willows that draped over it like mourners at a viewing. It was a hopeless ruin, but he could see what the place must have looked like in its heyday, back when the flaked paint had been fresh and the high imposing Doric pillars stood straight and tall.

Now everything sagged, wings and cupolas giving way to gravity, and the entire structure seemed to be sinking slowly into the Southern soil. It was as if Tommy McClane and his son had devoted all their energy to the town's Historical Society, but at the expense of maintaining their own family homestead.

There was a light on back in the house—dimly visible through the broad windows—and a lamp hanging on the porch, its flame flickering in the thick evening breeze.

Parking next to a big black Ford Ranger, they got out and

looked up at the long porch that ran along the entire front of the house. Two figures were sitting there, gazing back down at them, lit only by lamp light. He could smell the rich mossy odor of the swamp somewhere nearby.

"Mr. McClane?" Sam called up.

"Sam," Tommy said. "Glad you decided to take me up on the invitation."

They walked up the creaking front steps to where Tommy and Nate were sitting on cane-backed chairs. Both had been reading, Sam saw. Tommy held Tony Hurwitz's *Confederates in the Attic,* while Nate was gazing raptly down at what Sam realized was an electronic reader. It cast a ghostly light on his features.

"Kid's a reader, what can I say?" Tommy asked, by way of explanation. "When I was his age I was reading Batman comics. But he asked for a reader for his birthday, and now I can't get him to put it down."

"Tommy, this is my brother Dean," Sam said.

"Pleased to meet you," Tommy said, holding out a hand.

"Quite a place you've got here," Dean said, accepting the handshake.

"Been in my family for five generations. We were gonna sell, but then the bottom dropped out of the real estate market, so I guess we're stuck here."

"What are you reading there?" Dean asked the boy.

Nate grinned a little sheepishly, held up the reader so Dean could see. *Hammer of the Gods.*

Dean's eyebrows went up.

"You like Zeppelin?"

"I tried to get the kid to listen to Allmans, Skynyrd..." Tommy shook his head. "Lost cause."

"Zeppelin's the best," the boy said. "I'm reading the part where they're partying in the Riot House in L.A., throwing furniture down into the pool."

Dean nodded.

"You know half the stuff in that book is bullcrap."

"Yeah, but it's still pretty good."

"Yeah." Dean grinned. "It is."

"You want a glass of iced tea?" Tommy asked, nodding to the Mason jars sitting on the table beside them. "Or something stronger? I got beer in the fridge."

"Wouldn't say no," Dean said.

"Help yourself. It's straight back through the door, last room on the right."

Dean opened the screen door. Stepping inside, he was immediately struck by the sheer size of the house around him, an ancient and somehow majestic shipwreck of a mansion that was much too large for the man and his son. The rooms he could see were lavishly appointed with worn furnishings, tables and lamps and Georgian antiques that looked like they could've sold at auction for thousands.

He wondered if anything significant had changed since the McClanes' ancestors had lived there.

Passing through the arched kitchen doorway, he opened the fridge and took out a bottle of Beck's. Turning, he glanced up and noticed the broom above the door.

And froze.

What the hell...?

There was a small cloth bag mounted over the doorway he'd just stepped through. And another, nailed up over the window to his immediate right. In fact, from where he stood, he could see that every point of entry was marked with some small, easily overlooked item—a bundle of chicken bones tied together with hair, a scrap of rawhide wrapped around a bunch of feathers and animal teeth.

You idiot. You walked right into this. Without so much as a knife to protect yourself—

Slowly, without making a sound, Dean set the unopened beer on the counter. He felt wide-awake, absolutely alert. Walking silently back in the direction he'd come, he automatically started evaluating all possible exits and weapons.

By the time he got to the screen door and heard Tommy McClane laughing, his heart was beating fast.

What happened next would depend on how hard McClane wanted things to be for him.

"What people don't realize about a battle like Bull Run," Tommy was saying, "was how much the original eyewitness reports of what happened—"

He stopped, as Dean stepped up from behind.

"Don't move," Dean muttered over his shoulder, and he tossed the Impala keys to Sam. "Get the car and bring it around. Knife's in the usual place. Get it."

"Dean, wait."

"There's hex bags all through here. Place is a freaking death trap."

"Dean, wait." Sam stood up. "The McClanes aren't possessed," he said. "It's hoodoo."

"Those charms you saw are household protection symbols," Tommy said, sounding surprisingly calm. Looking back at Dean, he scowled a little incredulously. "Were you actually gonna stab me with my own barbecue fork?"

"It was the only thing I could find," Dean mumbled, laying it aside, then turned to Sam. "What else did you forget to tell me?"

"You were already suspicious. I didn't want to make it worse."

"Yeah, well..." Dean fumed. "I left my beer inside." As he stepped back into the house, he thought he could feel McClane's eyes burning into his back.

Gotta be my imagination, he thought. *That's just a stupid cliché.*

When he got back to the porch, Nate had switched off his e-book, and he and Sam were listening to Tommy McClane's theory of how the South really lost the war.

"This business with the noose," McClane said, "that's just part of it. By the last year of the war, Lee's armies were desperate. Soldiers were using all kinds of Louisiana voodoo on the battlefield. Hell, in the end, the CSA practically sanctioned it. Benign stuff at first... charms for protection and herbal remedies. Brought over by the slave trade, absorbed across the color line into local culture, including the poor white farm boys who were out there dying on the front lines.

"And by that point, the Confederates were using everything they could to try to hold off the Union." He shook his head. "Except it was backfiring all over the place. Here in Mission's Ridge, for example, in the battle they're re-enacting this week, the South was winning. And then all of a sudden, without any explanation, Confederate troops started turning on each other, and on themselves. The history books treat it like it was some kind of insurrection, a fatal breakdown in the chain of command. But it was more than that. It was a damn massacre and the town fell to the North because of it."

"Let me guess," Dean said. "Jubal Beauchamp was right smack in the middle."

"And he was wearing the noose," McClane said. "No doubt in my mind."

"So where is it now?" Sam asked.

Tommy McClane looked up at them wearily.

"Wherever it is," he said, "good riddance. There's a reason why I've got protection charms over every door and window in my house."

"Have you ever heard of something called Moa'ah?" Dean asked.

Tommy flinched visibly at the mention of it.

"Where did you hear about that?"

"Let's just say I got to see some of it up close and personal," Dean said.

"That's impossible. If you came across the Moa'ah, you

wouldn't be sitting around talking about it."

"Well, I had help."

"You really think it's that powerful?" Sam asked.

"It's inside the noose." Every trace of good humor had fallen away from McClane's face. "And those knots were tied in Hell."

TEN

Their motel room was painted blue and gray.

Half of it was decorated with old photos of Union soldiers and paintings of the Yankees. The other half was decorated with Rebel flags and replicas of Confederate artifacts. An imaginary Mason-Dixon Line divided the space cleanly between two sagging single beds.

"You want Lee or Sherman?" Sam asked.

"Huh?"

"North or South?"

Dean didn't answer, just climbed on one of the beds and lay on his back with his hands locked behind his head, staring straight up at the ceiling fan as it paddled the humid night air.

After a moment of silence, Sam set up the laptop on the desk and went online, running an image search on different types of nooses. In the quiet, he could feel the slow tension boiling off his brother until finally it became something he could no longer ignore.

Sam turned around and looked at Dean.

"Dean? Is there something you need to say to me?"

Dean didn't move. "Nope."

"So you're just going to lie there and watch the fan spin all night?"

"I was thinking about brushing my teeth."

"Come on. If you internalize one more dark thought, you're going to explode."

Dean sat up fast, the shadows under his eyes making him look simultaneously exhausted and bursting with nervous energy.

"Your buddy McClane talks about Hell like he did time there. Meanwhile I could give him a freakin' guided tour of the place."

"He knows about the noose," Sam said.

"And that's another thing. What *does* he really know? History's not my strong point, and personally I could give two craps about who lost the war and why. I'm here to smoke this thing, whatever it is, and get out of Dodge."

"It's not that simple." Sam stood up from the desk. "What's this really about? McClane or me?"

Dean stopped pacing and faced him across the room.

"It used to be about us, Sammy. You and me and Bobby, and that's it. Now it's you and me and whoever you feel like trusting on any given day. And frankly I'm not so crazy about that."

"Well, it's a little late to cut him out," Sam said. "So for the sake of getting this figured out, let's focus."

Sitting back down at the computer, he added, "Take a look at this."

He clicked back to the digitized image of Jubal Beauchamp that showed the hangman's knot around his neck. Dean stepped up beside him and stood, arms crossed, peering down.

"Beauchamp's rope had six coils around it, the standard technique. Right?"

"Sure."

"It says here that the more loops you make, the more the friction increases on the rope."

"So?"

"But if you look at this picture—" Sam magnified the Beauchamp image, squinting at the grainy pixels. Centering on the noose, he looked closer. "there's a seventh coil."

"Riveting. Really." Dean returned to the bed. "So where does that get us?"

"We need to go out there in the morning and talk to Oiler again. Find out *exactly* what he saw—what happened at the wedding. He has to be holding something back."

"And this time he'll definitely tell us the truth."

"No," Sam said, "he'll prevaricate and lie and try to cover up, just like everyone else is doing. But we're going to lean on him—just you and me—until he levels with us." He turned and faced the bed. "Because I, for one, am sick of feeling like we're not getting the whole story here."

Dean studied his brother's face, saw cold steel in his eyes

and wanted to believe in it.

"And then what?"

"And then we find this thing," Sam said, "and we deal with it."

Dean didn't say anything.

Sam closed his eyes and listened to the silence.

Far off in the distance he heard the scream of a train whistle.

ELEVEN

Outside of town, night fell over the battlefield, its full weight sinking fast over the star-rattled sky.

Campfires dotted the hillside where the men bivouacked, re-enactors on both sides hunkered in front of their tents, drinking from tin cups, scraping food off plates, talking in the hushed tones of men away from their families and homes. Corncob pipes were produced, muskets disassembled and lovingly cleaned and oiled by lantern-light, the old rituals brought out and pored over one more time.

Here and there cell phones shone between the trees like blue fireflies as one man or another sneaked a quiet call to a wife or girlfriend.

Private Terry Johnson sat in front of the fire with his banjo, plucking out the first plaintive notes of 'My Old Kentucky Home.' He played softly, almost to himself, unselfconsciously. It was late now, and most of the 32nd had already bunked down for the night in preparation for the long march in the morning.

The only other sounds were the crackling of the fire and the nickering of the several dozen horses corralled near the cavalry troops, as the animals too settled down for the night.

"Know any Coldplay?"

Johnson flinched a little in surprise and stopped plucking. Phil Oiler—also known as Norwalk Pettigrew, of the 32nd Georgia—sat down on a stump next to him.

"Oh," he said. "Hey, Phil."

"Call me Norrie." Oiler leaned his musket against one of the big stones that formed the fire-pit and brought out his bayonet, wiping it with a chamois. "That was my guy's nickname."

"Cool." Johnson started to put the banjo aside, and Oiler stopped him.

"No, man, keep playing. In the camps that was what kept the men's spirits up." Reaching into his jacket, he brought out a dented metal flask, removed the cap and held it out. "Whiskey?"

"Thanks." Johnson tipped it back and took a sip, letting it burn. It was good, smooth stuff, probably not what the boys on the battlefield had sipped a hundred and fifty years earlier, but who knew? This was the South, after all. Maybe it was even better then.

"Much appreciated."

"That's an authentic Civil War flask, by the way," Oiler said. "1860s."

"Pretty cool."

"Set me back a pretty penny, but it's worth it." He fell silent, regarding the flask in the firelight. "You know any more songs?"

"Just a handful, really. 'Foggy Mountain Breakdown,' and the first part of 'The Rainbow Connection,' that's about it."

Oiler sighed and placing the bayonet on a piece of cloth sat back in the flickering firelight.

After a moment of silence, Johnson picked listlessly at the banjo while casting about for something to say. He was relatively new to the 32nd, having only joined up a few months earlier, after his wife left him for some orthodontist that she'd met online. The loneliness had driven him to seek out men with similar interests. He didn't know Oiler very well, except that the man sold insurance and had a family somewhere in Atlanta.

Oiler, for his part, didn't seem to mind the silence. He passed the flask back again, nodding his encouragement, and Johnson took another pull of whiskey. All around them the night intensified, gaining bulk and breadth until the hillside and trees and everything outside the campfire's immediate glow was rendered in varying shades of blackness.

"Almost *feels* like 1863," Oiler said, "doesn't it? So still..."

"Yeah."

"Here, let me show you something," Oiler said. He sounded different now, his voice soft and strange. The fire crackled and popped hypnotically in front of them.

"What is it?" Johnson asked.

Oiler didn't answer right away. For a moment the flames guttered low, dropping them into near-total darkness.

When the fire brightened again, Johnson thought he saw something around the other man's neck, just for an instant. Then it was gone, a trick of the shadows. He rubbed his eyes.

It has to be the whiskey, he thought. *I'm seeing things.*

"Phil..."

"Call me Norrie." Oiler was smiling now. "Did you see it?"

"Did I see... what?"

"I know more about Jubal Beauchamp than what I let on," Oiler said. "A lot more."

"You mean Dave?"

Oiler shook his head and smiled.

"He let me try it on for myself, you know—around my own neck. And it felt *good*."

Johnson stood up a little unsteadily. Maybe he was drunker than he thought.

It was time for bed.

"Where do you think you're going?" Oiler's voice asked gently.

"I—I'm just—"

Sudden, shocking pain exploded through his foot, erupting up his leg. Looking down, he saw that Oiler had jammed his bayonet down through his boot, impaling his foot directly into the ground.

Before Johnson could even scream or get loose, Oiler yanked the blade free and landed on top of him, clapping a hand over his mouth and pinning him to the ground, holding him in the dirt with the full weight of his body.

Johnson fought to get free, but Oiler was too strong. One of them kicked over the banjo in the struggle, knocking it into the fire where it emitted sour little *blunks* and *twangs*. Then Oiler's face was right next to his, close enough that he could feel the other man's chin-stubble scrape against his cheek and smell the whiskey on his breath.

There's no noose around his neck, Johnson thought dizzily. *There's nothing there at all.*

"War is hell," Oiler whispered in his ear.

He seemed impossibly strong, an instrument of coiled muscle. Vaguely, through his agony, Johnson realized that smells were pouring off the other man's skin in waves: alcohol, tobacco, and something else, the stink of a moldy old cellar. "Welcome to it."

"Please," Johnson muttered into the other man's palm.

"Put this in your mouth."

"What?"

"You heard me."

Johnson looked down and saw the bayonet poised just below his chin.

"Please. No."

Oiler slammed the blade's tip upward, cracking Johnson's teeth. He gagged as the oily metal invaded his mouth, pain spiking deep as the sharpened edge sliced through his lips and tongue. His sinuses began to fill with salty warmth. All his life he'd wondered what went through men's minds as they faced death. Now he understood.

His thoughts circled back to his parents and his estranged wife and his sister in New Jersey, and all the things he'd never done and would never get to do. He tried to talk but his lips couldn't form the words beyond a few desperate whining sounds. Tears flooded his eyes, spilling down his cheeks.

Above him, the stars had lost their shape—they shivered and streamed like mad planets against the outer wall of a universe that no longer made any sense.

Still pinning him, Oiler whispered something, speaking words in some other language that Johnson couldn't understand.

He felt the blade jerk forward.

And then nothing.

TWELVE

Sam and Dean awoke to the wail of police sirens coming from somewhere outside the motel room, howling down the pre-dawn streets of Mission's Ridge. Dean climbed out of bed and drew back the heavy curtains to reveal daylight just starting to raise a bleary eyelid on the horizon.

"That's never good," he said, and he glanced at Sam. "This is supposed to be a quiet little burg."

"Sounds like they're heading west."

Dean nodded.

"I'm thinking the battleground." He nodded toward the bathroom. "You want the first shower?"

"Go ahead."

Moving with practiced efficiency, they got dressed in their FBI suits and went out to the Impala. Pulling onto the road, they headed west, stopping at a convenience store for coffee on the way. Twenty minutes later they swung up into the parking lot outside the battlefield. The sky overhead was a bloody, cloud-streaked ruin with mile-long bars of darkness and bronze raked across it from horizon to horizon.

"We should've come out here last night," Sam said.

Dean gulped a scalding mouthful of coffee.

"Would it have made a difference?"

They got out and started walking across the dew-damp grass. Through the early morning mist, Sam could already see the yellow tape flapping around the tents of the 32nd Georgia. Confederate and Union re-enactors milled outside the police barricades, trying to get a look at the crime scene.

Dean pulled one of the Confederate soldiers off to the side, away from the rest, while Sam tried to see what was happening beyond the crush of bystanders. Just as he was ready to give up, Dean stepped back over.

"One of the guys found 'em out there when he got up to drain the snake," he said. "That was about an hour ago. They'd been lying out there most of the night. Phil Oiler and friend."

"Damn."

Pushing through the crowd, they waved their badges at a cop who was about to protest, then made their way through the rows of blue-and-red flashing emergency vehicles lining the edge of the hillside. Approaching the tent, they stepped over the tape and walked toward the two long gray bags sitting on either side of the darkened fire-pit.

Sheriff Daniels was hunched over one of the body bags, zipping it up. The expression on her face was one of stiff and implacable distaste.

"Sheriff?" Sam called out.

She didn't bother looking up at them. State police and local emergency medical technicians were re-directing foot-traffic, ordering people back in the loud impersonal voices of those who did these things for a living. There was a sharp click from overhead, and a voice—heavy with Southern twang—came from the loudspeakers that were mounted along the perimeter.

"Attention. This is Sergeant Earl Ray Harris of the Georgia State Police. Due to the events of last night, the rest of the re-enactment has been canceled. Please gather your belongings in an orderly fashion and vacate the premises immediately."

Why the hell would they do that? Sam wondered. *This is still an active crime scene...*

A communal groan came from the hundreds of men bivouacked out on the hillside, and the groups began to dissipate. Looking back at the crime scene, Sam saw Sheriff Daniels coming toward him carrying a canvas tote bag.

"Sheriff—"

"Not now." She pushed past them without breaking stride, the bag swinging at her side. As it nudged her leg, Dean thought he heard something inside making a clinking sound.

"Come on," Dean said, nodding at the bodies by the fire-pit. "Before they haul them off."

He and Sam approached the EMTs just as they were placing the body bags on stretchers, and Dean badged them with a perfunctory flick of the wrist.

"Federal Agents Townes and Van Zandt. Mind if we take a quick look?" Without waiting for permission, he pulled the zipper down on the nearest bag, widening it until he could make out the face inside. It was a man in his early twenties, with dried blood splashed around his mouth and chin like some grotesque attempt at clown makeup, his blank eyes bugged open almost comically in butcher-shop burlesque.

"You recognize this guy?" he asked his brother.

"No," Sam responded. "But I know this one."

Dean glanced at the second body, and immediately identified the man as Oiler, the bull-shouldered re-enactor they'd interviewed the previous day.

"My guess," one of the EMTs was saying, "is that Oiler stabbed Johnson, then cut his own throat. Must have kept it quiet, commando-style. Nobody in the tent heard any screams."

"Got an extra set of gloves?" Sam asked, and the EMT tossed him a pair. Sam reached down and turned Oiler's head sideways.

"Dean?"

"Yeah?"

"Check it out."

Dean squatted down next to him, and they both looked at the red rope-burns around what was left of Oiler's neck.

"Was there something around his neck when you found him?" Sam asked the technician. "A rope or something?"

"Not that we saw," the EMT said. "But we just got here. The sheriff was on the scene for half an hour before we arrived. You might want to ask her."

"That's a heck of an idea," Dean said, and stood up, looking at Sam. "You ready?"

Sam nodded. But he was gazing off into the middle distance, where a group of figures in Confederate uniforms were hitching a wheeled cannon to the back of a Ford Bronco. Glancing around, he prodded one of the re-enactors standing beside him.

"What are those guys hooking up to their truck?

The man squinted.

"Looks like a siege howitzer. It's a rifled-cannon."

"What's it shoot?"

"The real thing? Whatever you put in it. Solid shot, grape, canister, shell, even chain shot—that's two balls connected by a chain. Like getting slammed head-on with the devil's own hairy beanbag." The man sounded envious. "We're talking badass." He shook his head. "'Course, that one up there wouldn't fire a thing."

"So it's a replica?"

The re-enactor snorted.

"Let's hope so. Otherwise they'd be driving off with an authentic wartime relic. That's a Federal offense—but you know all about that, don't'cha." He gestured back at the crime scene, where the EMTs were picking up the stretchered bodies. "Can you believe this?"

"Guess I have to," Sam said. "Are you leaving?"

"No way. None of us are. Not until we find out who did this." The re-enactor met Sam's gaze, and Sam saw deep determination there, as if the man and his fellow soldiers were genuinely at war. "Some of those guys were my friends."

"Sam!" Dean shouted, already halfway to the parking lot. "You coming or what?"

Sam went after him. When he looked back at the battlefield, the men in gray were hooking a second howitzer up to the back of a pickup truck.

THIRTEEN

Reporters were already clustered in front of the sheriff's office when Sam and Dean got back into town. The only available parking was two blocks away, between two TV news vans. Backing the Impala toward the curb, Dean checked the rearview mirror and saw Castiel sitting in the back seat, looking at him.

He jumped a little reflexively and slammed on the brakes.

"Damn it, Cass, how many times do I have to tell you, don't *do* that." Sam jerked round in his seat.

"You have to get out of here," Castiel said.

"What? *Why?*"

"There's some extremely heavy demonic activity gathering in the area. You both need to be as far away from it as possible."

"Right," Dean growled, "running from demons, 'cuz that's *exactly* how we roll."

"You don't understand." Castiel sat forward, gripping the seatback with both hands until Dean could hear the springs in the upholstery creaking. He spoke with an intensity that made each word hiss like molten iron plunged in cold water. "I thought I could identify the source of the Moa'ah. But you've been drawn back here as a trap. The Witness is closer than ever."

"Judas, right?" Sam asked. "That is who we're talking about, isn't it."

"Yes," Castiel admitted.

"Then why didn't you say so before."

The angel shook his head.

"At first it didn't make sense, that so powerful a Witness would be involved in a simple local skirmish."

"And now it does?"

"Judas is the custodian of the noose. He and his minions are compelled to be here in Mission's Ridge because someone has reactivated the noose's power. And they are not happy about it."

"How do you know all this?" Sam asked.

"The knowledge was placed in my head."

"By...?"

Castiel regarded him with absolute earnestness.

"By the only one capable of such things, I presume. God Himself."

"You know, Cass, God's told a lot of crazy people to do a lot of crazy things, and some of 'em aren't so nice."

"There's more."

"Swell."

"You're not the one they want." Castiel turned to focus on Sam. "Whoever's behind this is forcing your hand, Sam. Using the Judas noose to speed up the Apocalypse clock.

They're trying to create a situation where you have no choice but to become Lucifer's vessel."

Before Sam could respond, Dean spoke up again.

"Of course, the Almighty didn't bother telling you *how* this is gonna happen, did he?" he said.

"No."

"Sounds more and more like Him all the time." Dean glanced at his brother. "You ready?"

Sam nodded.

"Dean, wait," the angel said, his voice almost pleading.

"Sorry, Cass. Never been good at that."

He and Sam climbed out of the Impala and started walking up the sidewalk toward the crowded entrance of the sheriff's office.

"You realize he's probably right," Sam said, without looking over at his brother.

"Uh-huh."

"But we're going in anyway."

"You got an issue with that?"

Sam shook his head.

"If they want me bad enough, they'll just come after me anyway."

"So we hit first," Dean said, "and hit hard."

They arrived at the entrance to the sheriff's office and pushed through a throng of reporters and spectators gathered outside the entryway. The door itself was locked.

Dean took out his badge and rapped it sharply on the glass. From inside, the sheriff's deputy—a paunchy man with a cartoonishly thick black moustache—looked up at them then down at their badges. He came over and unlocked the door.

"Sheriff here?" Dean asked, as they slipped inside.

"Yeah, but you don't want to interrupt her right now."

"It's important," Dean said. Across the office he could already see Daniels at her desk, phone clamped to one ear, almost yelling into the receiver.

"I don't give a damn *what* they're telling you," she was saying, "I want them cleared off that battlefield *now*. Those men are contaminating my crime scene."

"*Your* crime scene?" Dean strode up to the desk and stared at her until she was forced to look up and acknowledge him. Then she just turned away, trying to find somewhere else to fix her attention.

Dean moved with her, holding eye contact. She glared back at him, and finally ended the conversation, hanging up the phone.

"What do you want?" she demanded.

"Where's the noose?"

"The *what?*"

"Phil Oiler was wearing a rope around his neck when he died last night, and now it's gone. You were the only one around before the EMTs showed up. You've been withholding information this whole time. So *where's the noose?*"

The sheriff's face went very white, except for a red patch on either cheek. Her lips tightened, and Dean could see a small blood vessel throbbing high up on one side of her forehead.

"Get out of my office," she gritted.

"Not yet." Dean didn't move.

The vein in her head pulsed harder.

"I've got two hundred Civil War re-enactors refusing to pack up and let me do my job out there. I don't need you two clowns making things worse."

"We're not leaving until we get some answers," Dean said.

"Oh, I'm getting answers. In fact..." Her lips turned slightly, forming into a thin and totally humorless smile, "I've got the Atlanta field office of the FBI calling me back right now. That *is* where you two said that you were from, isn't it?"

"Yeah," Dean said, "but—"

The phone on Daniels' desk started ringing again.

"Here we are." She picked it up. "Hello? Yes sir. This is Mission's Ridge Sheriff Jacqueline Daniels calling. Sorry to bother you, but I've got two men here claiming to be Federal Agents, and I just wanted to verify their identification."

"Wait," Sam said. "Let me talk to them."

"Not a chance." Daniels shook her head and turned her back to them. "Yes, sir. Agents Townes and Van Zandt. That's right, V-A-N Z-A-N-D-T. Thanks. I'll wait."

Sam glanced at Dean, and saw that his brother was staring straight at the sheriff.

Except he *wasn't*.

He was actually staring at a nylon tote bag that rested in the corner of the office. It was the same one Daniels had carried away from the crime scene. Dean was staring straight at it, as if he could somehow see inside through sheer force of will, or levitate it into the air.

Daniels smiled, and spoke into the phone again.

"Yes, sir. I appreciate that. Thank you for your time." She shook her head. "Jerry?" she shouted.

The paunchy deputy who had let them in came around the corner.

"What's up, Sheriff?"

"Please escort these two men to the holding cell. The charge is posing as a law-enforcement official." She smiled again, this time directly at Dean. "We'll have plenty of time to figure out who they are later. Meanwhile they can rot in the drunk tank." She glanced out of the window. "And haul their piece of crap car to the impound lot. I don't want it cluttering up my street."

"Whoa!" Dean snapped, a sudden rush of anger rising in his face. "Watch your damn mouth, lady. You can't just—"

Jerry pivoted on them with unexpected intensity. His paunchy, thickly moustached face didn't look soft or easy-going anymore. A new type of hardness had spread over his expression now, and his hand was resting on the butt of his sap.

"Easy or hard, gentlemen. Makes no difference to me."

"Okay," Dean said, "look..."

"Hard it is, then," Jerry said, drawing the club from his belt. Suddenly he looked like a man who enjoyed using it on vagrants, bums, and anyone else who got in his way, whenever he had the chance.

"Wait!" Sam said, holding up his hands, palms out.

That was all he managed to get out before a bomb burst across the sky. It shook the windows of the sheriff's office as it exploded.

FOURTEEN

The explosion caught Sheriff Daniels and her deputy completely off-guard. They both spun around in reaction to the noise.

Dean saw Jerry lowering the sap, and that was all the opportunity he needed.

"Come on!" he shouted. Barging past the deputy, he sprinted out of the office, through the lobby, and out the door. Sam was close behind.

The front steps of the sheriff's building were still cluttered with reporters and camera crews, but they were all facing the other way, toward the outskirts of town, where a second roaring explosion had just gone off, spitting aftershocks across the horizon.

"What is that?" Sam shouted.

Dean jabbed a finger off beyond the low buildings of downtown Mission's Ridge. The sun was up now, and lay behind them.

"It's coming from out by the battlefield."

Scrambling down the sidewalk, he bolted across the street and down the block to where the Impala sat waiting, then jumped behind the wheel almost without waiting to see if Sam had made the trip along with him.

But Sam was already there, climbing into the passenger seat.

Dean gunned it, and the Impala's engine roared to life with a reassuring throb that seemed to say, *What took you so long?* Its wheels laid sizzling parabolas of rubber across the concrete as the car spun forward and went shooting off toward the outskirts of town.

Behind him, Dean could already see blue and white lights swirling in the rear-view mirror.

"Looks like them Duke boys are fixing to get themselves in a heap of trouble again," he muttered in his best Merle Haggard drawl.

Sam checked his side-view mirror.

"Can't you drive any faster?"

Dean grinned.

"No. But I can do *this*." He threw the wheel hard to the right, sluicing the Impala's back-end around at a ninety-degree angle, sending them straight into the 'Dixie Boy Buggie Wash.' One of the attendants—a skinny guy in a lawn chair—jumped out of the way far enough for Dean to drive completely into the car wash. Water and wet sponges splashed off the windshield, enveloping the car, and Dean craned his neck enough to watch the sheriff's cruiser go flying up Main Street in the direction of the explosions.

"I think we lost 'em." Another explosion echoed off in the distance. "And here I thought the re-enactment was canceled."

"I don't think this is a re-enactment," Sam offered.

"Then what the hell..." Dean stared, looking over, and the words faded on his lips. His brother was holding a small, bloodstained leather satchel on his lap, tugging loose the strip of rawhide that acted as its drawstring. "What's *that*?"

Sam held it up.

"I snagged it out of the sheriff's tote bag on the way out the door."

"Not bad, Sammy," Dean said. "Did you happen to see the noose in there, too?"

"I didn't exactly have time to look."

"Crap."

Dean pulled out of the car wash, waved to the attendant on the other side, and slammed the accelerator again, sending the Impala shrieking around the narrow alleyway.

"Man, that bag *stinks*. What's in there, anyway?"

"Check it out." Sam removed a tarnished silver coin, holding it up to examine its markings.

"Confederate?"

Sam shook his head.

"Older than that, I think." He took out his phone and snapped a picture of it. "I'll send it to Bobby and see if he can help identify some of the markings."

He did so, then continued, "Judging from these bloodstains, and the fact that this leather smells like gastric bile—"

"I'm not even gonna *ask* how you know that—"

"—I'm guessing it came from somewhere inside one of those bodies out on the battlefield," Sam finished.

"So what, the rope-curse sends you psycho, then *pays* you for it?"

"Yup."

"Crazy."

"Dean! Look!" Sam pointed up ahead, perhaps a mile into the distance, where a huge cloud of black smoke was rising up into the sky. "Still think it's a re-enactment?"

"We gotta get out there."

"If the sheriff sees us..."

"I think she's got her hands full right now," Dean said, and he floored it.

BOOM!

Another explosion rocked the earth underneath them as they jumped out of the Impala and chased their shadows across the parking lot. Sirens were rising up all around them in the distance. The smoke was already thick enough to sting their eyes and make their noses water.

In front of them, the entire Mission's Ridge battleground seemed to be on fire. Men in Confederate and Union uniforms—hundreds of them—were scurrying in all directions, heading away from burning tents and enormous smoking craters that had opened up in the well-manicured grass like giant angry mouths.

The police cruisers in the parking lot were dispensing local cops and state troopers, the officers yelling into radios and trying to be heard above the chaos.

"The shooting," Dean shouted, "where's it coming from?"

Sam pointed across the creek and up the hillside, perhaps a thousand yards in the distance. At the top of the hill, a row of SUVs and pickup trucks were parked overlooking the gorge below. Standing alongside them was a phalanx of siege howitzers like the ones that they had seen earlier. Two figures in uniform—at least they seemed to be in uniform— were packing ordnance into the rifled cannons.

"Look out!" He winced as one of the howitzers blasted, its projectile shrieking downward over the hillside and across the creek, where it slammed into the earth with a deafening *BOOM*! Great chunks of rock, dirt, and splintered tree roots sprayed up into the air and came showering down everywhere.

"I thought they were *replicas*!" Dean shouted.

"They are!"

"Then how—"

THOOM! Another shell slammed close enough that Sam actually felt the ground lurch up and go sideways under his feet. Before he knew it he was on his knees, his mouth and nose clogged with soil and flecks of stone.

When his vision cleared, Dean was hauling him to his feet, brushing him off, yanking him back.

"You okay, Sammy?"

"I'm all right," he managed, wiping a stream of blood from his eyes. He was weak, dazed—the pores of his skin felt like they'd been packed with flying debris—his first instinct was to find safety, but running away wasn't an option right now, and he knew it.

"We're gonna get killed out here!" Dean shouted. "They're shooting at us!"

"I don't think so."

"What are you talking about?"

Sam spun around, regaining his bearings, trying to take in the full scope of what was happening around him—to make it make sense somehow. Groups of re-enactors were streaming in every direction, trying to find their way back to the parking lot through the clouds of flying dirt and dust.

Up ahead, the corral of cavalry division horses were going wild with panic, bucking and trying to get free from their pen.

There were some binoculars lying in the grass next to a tent, and he scooped them up. Bringing them to his eyes, he squinted until the details came into view.

And he saw them.

The men loading the howitzers were indeed dressed in uniform, some Confederate, others Union. As Sam stared at them, they seemed to sense that they were being watched, and one of them turned and looked right back at him.

The man grinned.

His eyes flicked to total black.

The cannons roared again, three at a time now, filling the air with an explosion so loud that it seemed to blot out every other sound on earth.

"Damn it, Sam, we have to go *now*!" Dean screamed at him, but this time Sam hardly heard him. "They're gonna blow us up!"

"That's the least of it," Sam said. "They're demons."

"*What?*"

"See for yourself." He thrust the binoculars at Dean and waited while he stared through them.

Then Dean seemed to become very calm. He reached backward under his shirt, drawing a blade from its sheath.

"How many, you think?"

"Three, maybe four."

"Two each?"

"Sounds good."

"You want the blade?"

"No, I'm good." Sam shook his head. "You take it." Dean frowned.

"You're not gonna go all 'Dark Sam' on me, right?"

"*What?*"

"Sorry. Too soon?"

"Dean—"

"Fine." Dean nodded. "I get it. We're good."

Sam shook his head. He honestly couldn't tell how serious his brother's queries were. And at the moment he didn't care. He was simply—almost absurdly—relieved to have Dean fighting alongside him.

Tromping uphill through the choking cloud of smoke, with artillery rounds booming through the landscape below them like some cataclysmic percussion instrument, Sam almost lost sight of where he was going. Above them artillery rounds pierced the air. For a span of several minutes it seemed like every few yards he gained, another explosion sent him skidding back down the embankment, until he had to sink his fingers into the earth and claw his way to the top.

Glancing over his shoulder, he caught a brief glimpse of the battlefield below. Ambulances had arrived in the parking lot, their roof-lights pulsing through the airborne debris. Cops and paramedics were moving forward between the craters, trying to get the injured re-enactors out of harm's way. Nobody seemed to be in charge, and if they were, nobody else seemed able to understand them.

Near the top, Sam and Dean stopped and fell motionless, gasping hard for what little air there was close to the ground. Sam's ribs ached from the exertion. From here he was looking straight up at the undersides of the cannons, each one recoiling violently as it fired another round. He glanced over, trying to gauge his brother's state of mind.

Dean's face looked flush but triumphant—in his mind he'd already won this battle, or perhaps he was just happy to be fighting demons instead of bureaucratic red tape.

"How do you want to...?" Sam started, but Dean was already in motion, springing up over the top.

Scrambling to follow him, Sam was just in time to see his brother dive forward and plant Ruby's demon-killing blade into the first of the fusiliers.

The demon sparked and flashed white, its meat-suit collapsing. Yanking the blade loose, Dean whipped around and flattened the soldier behind him with a roundhouse Billy-Jack kick. Even on its back, though, the thing was faster than Dean was, springing upright and grabbing hold of his leg, jolting Dean forward.

The blade went spinning into the grass.

Sam grabbed the knife and drove it straight down into the demon's skull. The bone burst like crockery and it fell howling to the ground, vomiting up shrieks of rage and agony as it flashed out, the blade sticking out of its head.

On the other side of the howitzers, the two remaining demons—one garbed as a Confederate, the other in a flat-crowned Union kepi—turned to charge them.

"I feel like we're fighting a Disneyland ride," Dean muttered, getting to his feet. "You still have the knife?"

Sam gaped at him. "I thought you picked it up."

The Confederate demon opened its mouth in a twisted, wide-jawed grin and lunged at Dean as if it intended to swallow him whole. Sam heard his brother let out an involuntary "uff!" of punched-out breath as the demon fell on top of him.

Behind him on the hillside, the siege howitzer that the demon had been loading stood ready to fire. Its fuse was hissing steadily down to the barrel. Vaguely—in a distracted, second-hand way—Sam noticed that it was gleaming with fresh blood.

"Sam Winchester?" a thick voice said.

Sam turned and saw the Union demon standing in front of him, holding the demon-knife.

"We're not interested in you," the demon said, with all the intensity of an IRS auditor going over a list of deductions. "Let us do our work here and we'll be on our way."

"What work is that?" Sam demanded.

When the demon didn't answer right away, Sam realized

that, for better or worse, he was going to have to act. He lunged for the demon, and it swung the knife at him in a scooping, desultory arc. Sam dodged left, recoiling, and felt the tip of the blade snag the fabric of his shirt as he sprinted around in front of the howitzer. The hillside dropped off sharply underneath his feet and he fell to his knees, starting to slide. But the Union demon kept its footing, raising the blade to deliver the killing blow.

"You should have stayed out of our way," the demon said. "It would have been much simpler."

Directly behind the demon, the howitzer roared. At the last second the thing seemed to realize what was happening, but it was too late. Sam shut his eyes as the entire upper half of the demon's body disappeared in a sulfurous spray, drenching him from above.

Sam reached up and, by sheer luck, caught the blade in mid-air. It was an astonishingly cool move, which of course meant that there was no way his brother could have seen it.

And Dean hadn't.

Because he was too busy getting the unholy snot beaten out of him by the last remaining demon on the hill.

Sam flung himself toward it. He could hear the faint gargling noises that his brother was making as the demon went about the business of strangling him.

Hearing him coming, the demon snapped around and glowered at Sam, onyx-eyed and seething with fury.

"You wouldn't dare intrude on this," he said, "if you knew the mission we were given."

Sam flicked his wrist, throwing the knife at the demon's face. The creature laughed and ducked easily, so that the blade went whistling over his head, landing in the dirt.

"We serve a greater purpose here." Releasing Dean, the demon stalked toward Sam, managing to look both heavy and impossibly graceful in its human meat-suit. "You're only one part of that."

"Yeah, well, you don't serve any purpose at all," Sam responded. He realized that he wasn't shouting anymore. He didn't have to. The guns had fallen silent.

From down below, a smell was rising up the hillside on the breeze. It was indescribably foul and rotten, as if tons of flyblown decaying flesh had been left out to bake in the sun.

"You wait," the demon told him. "Just wait. The way our numbers have waited, for so very long, suffering in the darkest hollows of—"

"Don't you ever *shut up*?" Dean shouted hoarsely from behind it, with what sounded like genuine exasperation. "You want us so bad, quit talking and kill us already!"

"An excellent idea, Dean Winchester."

The demon in the Union uniform pivoted and strode back toward him, taking two steps, then three, then freezing when it saw the ground beneath its feet, where Dean had used the knife to carve a Devil's Trap into the grass.

"Dumbass," Dean muttered, and he started muttering the exorcism rite.

FIFTEEN

After the exorcism, the smell of sulfur just got worse.

"Ugh, what did they open up down there?" Dean asked, gazing down between the howitzers at the smoldering battlefield below. He covered his nose and mouth with one hand and fanned the other in front of his face, as if he could somehow sweep a hole of clean air into the thick fumes that were accumulating around them.

"Smells like..."

"I know," Sam said. "And it's only getting worse."

Mortar shells from the cannons had torn the battlefield to shreds, uprooting trees and opening dozens of holes across the acreage. Through huge clouds of dirt and dust, he saw emergency personnel and state police—and probably the sheriff too, he thought glumly—gathered around one of the craters, peering down into it.

Long shafts of sunlight poked down from the clouds

above in almost palpable pillars, as if God himself was taking an interest in what had been unearthed there. Although it was hard to say from this distance, Dean thought he saw debris down inside the hole, mixed in with the rocks and roots of trees. And from the reactions of those standing around it, they seemed to be seeing it too.

He noticed something else, as well.

"Didn't that train used to be inside the shed?"

Sam looked down on the other side of the creek, to the steel rails that ran across the battleground. Far off to the left, an 1850s steam locomotive sat in front of a railway shed. Its engine, coal car, and caboose were in full view, as well as the artillery field piece, a Gatling gun mounted to the flatcar.

"Part of the re-enactment?" Dean asked hopefully.

"Then how come we didn't notice it before?" Sam countered. "Kind of hard to miss.

"That demon said he was serving a bigger purpose," he added. "I don't think they were trying to kill anybody. I think they were making holes. Trying to get down to what's in that hole in particular." He shrugged. "If they got those cannons working, who's to say they couldn't stoke up an old steam engine, as well?"

Dean was looking back out along the hillside, fixating on something in the middle distance.

"I want a closer look."

"The sheriff's down there," Sam said.

"So?"

"We're not FBI anymore, remember?"

"I've got a plan."

"Why doesn't that surprise me?"

"Hey." Dean clapped his shoulder. "Where's the trust?"

Sam was about to answer when he felt his phone vibrate in his back pocket.

"Hold on." He checked the screen. "It's Bobby."

"Not now."

"This could be important." Sam watched his brother rubbing his neck where the demon had tried to strangle him. "And are you really gonna tell me you couldn't use a breather?"

"Fine. Five minutes—tops." Sighing, Dean found a relatively secluded spot behind a pile of rocks and squatted down to watch the action below while Sam answered the call.

"Hey, Bobby."

"Sam?" Bobby didn't bother hiding his concern. "You sound winded, kid. Everything all right?"

"Dean and I just took out a demon kill-squad."

"Yeah, well, I got news about that."

"Go ahead."

"That coin you sent me a picture of," Bobby said, "is a shekel of Tyre—an ancient Phoenician coin. It's one of the thirty silver pieces that Judas got for betraying Christ. Where'd you get it?"

"Inside one of the victim's bodies," Sam said.

"Were you the one that found it?"

"I got it from the sheriff's office, but—"

"Sam, this is important. Did the sheriff know you took it?"

"I don't know. I don't think so. Why?"

"Did she ever try to stop you?"

Sam frowned.

"I'm not following you."

"It's blood money, Sam. There's only thirty coins like it in human history. It's payment for services rendered."

"What kind of services?"

Bobby's voice grew into an even more urgent growl.

"The lore says there's only way you earn that kind of silver. Same way Judas did. By betraying the people you love."

"So should I get rid of it?"

"You're not hearing me, Sam. It's a done deal. Wouldn't make a difference now if you did."

"Bobby..."

"I'll call you when I find out more," Bobby said. "In the meantime, you better let Dean know what he's up against."

"I will," Sam said. But when he looked back behind the rocks where his brother had been sitting, Dean was gone.

Sam made his way back down the hill. He found Dean squatting down behind the stands of cypress and live oak clustered along the creek, watching a Georgia State Police mobile crime lab that had pulled into the lot, finding its way between the clutter of other vehicles.

"What happened to you?" Sam asked, crouching down beside him.

"Just came down for a closer look." Dean glanced back at him, his expression unreadable. "What'd Bobby have to say?"

"The coin's two thousand years old." As he said these words, Sam realized he'd started to reach up and touch his collar, where his FBI agent's tie still hung loose around his neck. He consciously lowered his hand. "It confirms the Judas hypothesis that Cass was talking about."

"That's it?"

Sam let out a long sigh. "No. No, it isn't."

Dean looked back at his brother and narrowed his eyes.

"What going on, Sammy?"

"This is blood money." Sam reached into his pocket and pulled out the shekel. "Bobby says the only way anybody gets their hands on this..." The rest of the sentence was getting stuck somewhere in his chest, and he made himself finish it, "is by betraying someone you love."

Dean stared at him.

"I haven't done anything, Dean!"

"So maybe it's a down payment."

"What do you want me to say? You think I'm happy about this?"

"I think you're in over your head."

"So what, you want me to sit this one out? Handcuff myself to a tree till it's over?"

Dean turned away and shook his head, looking more exasperated than anything else.

"Is this part of that nightmare you had?"

"It might be," Sam said. "I still don't remember most of it." He stared down at the silver piece, then closed his fist around it and threw it as hard as he could into the creek, where it sparkled once and disappeared into the brown, slow-moving water.

For a silent moment they just sat there behind the trees, looking across the battleground and the parking lot, neither knowing what to say. The police forensics van reached the proximal end of the parking lot and was angling for a place to park. There was a tow-truck behind it, and Sheriff Daniels was directing it backward between the patrol cars, pickups, and civilian vehicles still filling the lot.

Watching all of this, and observing his brother out of the corner of his eye, it seemed to Sam that Dean was just waiting for an opportunity to move forward again and put this conversation behind them. If he had any more that he needed to say, now was the time.

"Dean..."

"Look," Dean broke in. "Don't get too hung up on it, okay? It doesn't necessarily mean anything." He stood up and brushed off his jeans. "Whatever happens between us, we'll deal with it then. Besides, you've still got a whole bag of those coins back in..." He stopped abruptly, galvanized by what he was staring at. "The *car*!"

"Dean, what—?"

"That *bitch*." Dean pointed at the parking lot where the tow-truck was hoisting the Impala up on its winch. Seconds later he was fighting his way through the trees. "She's towing my baby!"

"Dean, wait." Sam caught up and grabbed his brother's arm, holding him back. "Let's stay focused."

"Oh, I'm *so* focused," Dean said, straining against the grip.

"If you go running out there now, we'll both be in a holding cell in twenty minutes. You know that." Sam took hold of Dean's shoulders, holding his stare. "We'll get her back, okay? I promise."

"If there's so much as one scratch on her fender, I swear—"

"Okay, okay, got it." Sam nodded. "Now, you said you had a plan?"

Dean drew back and nodded across the river at the mobile crime unit. The technicians who climbed out of the back were garbed in heavy protective gear—suits, respirators and isolation masks that draped over their heads and shoulders like arc-welders' hoods.

"Those guys," he said. "That's where we start."

SIXTEEN

The disorganized crowd of police, civilians and re-enactors in the parking lot was still thick enough that Sam and Dean were able to approach the mobile crime lab undetected.

The lab technicians were already moving through the battlefield, and the state troopers and local police were busy evacuating the re-enactors and civilians. In all of the activity, nobody appeared to notice as Sam and Dean climbed into the back of the lab vehicle and procured two extra isolation suits and masks.

Sam grabbed two laminated ID badges by the lanyard and tossed one to Dean.

Dean looked at the name.

"How do you pronounce this—Cerasi?"

"Doesn't matter. They can't see our faces through here."

Lowering the biohazard hoods and eye-shields down over their eyes, Dean and Sam hopped down off the back of the truck. Dean looked behind, not entirely comfortable with the way the hood eclipsed his peripheral vision. He did a full three-sixty, still walking as he did so, and got a better view.

Along the western edge of the battlefield, a haphazard melange of media personalities, firemen, cops, and Civil War re-enactors were all clustered together watching the action. Surprisingly, and despite the overhead announcement by the state police, many of the soldiers didn't appear to have left after all.

With a jolt he backed into someone.

"Hey," a woman snapped, "watch where you're going, pal."

Dean looked up and saw that he'd walked right into the sheriff. The mask had hidden his face, and she hadn't recognized him.

"Sorry."

He and Sam kept walking until they reached the edge of the pit. Taking a deep breath through the air-purifier, Dean turned and looked down. More than one round must have struck the same spot, so the pit was deep.

It was a mass grave.

Forty feet below, ancient skeletons and bone-shards littered the inner walls of the pit everywhere they looked, along with chunks of shrapnel and rusty wartime ordnance. Here, a cannon barrel, there, a twisted mass that might have been a wagon. In the middle, a welter of ribs and spine segments and yellowish shafts that once had been a man. Dozens of men. Or more. The roots of trees were coiled among the last remains of the dead, knotting them in gnarled fists.

Squinting down into the hole, Dean Winchester's first reaction was pure relief, a sweeping sense of, *Oh. Is that all.* Not that any self-actualized aspect of him had honestly expected to find some depthless hellhole, a channel into the underworld, puking up brimstone and capering demonic atrocities lunging forward... or whatever... and yet—

And yet he had.

He *did.*

Because that was what he did after spending years down there, doing what he'd done.

He wondered.

He worried.

He feared.

Through sheer force of will, Dean shoved those notions aside—all of them—as far and as hard as he possibly could. Now more than ever he didn't want that experience contaminating the way he looked at the world... not that he had a choice.

Hell had been his Vietnam. It had stamped its mark on him for all eternity, and no amount of denial or self-imposed ignorance was going to change it.

Ever.

"Except this isn't Hell," he mumbled under his breath. "It's just a bunch of dead soldiers."

Suddenly that phrase, *dead soldiers*, struck him as improbably funny. He found himself imagining a pit littered with empty beer bottles, Pabst Blue Ribbon and Coors and perhaps the worst beer in America, Meister Brau. The tension cracked and he felt a welcome numbness spread over him in its place, stopping him where he stood.

A nearby police lab tech, mistaking his reaction for despair, gripped him by the shoulder.

"Steady on, man. First time's tough on all of us."

"Yeah," Dean managed, more grateful than ever that the mask hid his face. "It's tough all right."

"We're just here to do a job, right?"

"You got it, buddy."

"Hey, Dean." It was Sam, tapping him on the other shoulder. "Are you seeing this?"

"What part?"

"Over there."

Dean looked. The impromptu investigation team was lowering a sling and pulley contraption over the edge. Down below one of the workers was attaching it to an oblong box sticking halfway out of the dirt at the bottom of the crater. The box appeared to be made of iron. Unlike the other relics and debris in the pit, the passing century and a half didn't seem to have affected it much at all.

If anything, the metal appeared to be even shinier—more *luminous*—than it had any right to be. Seeing the thing gleaming, Dean imagined what it must have been like, buried under tons of dirt for decade after decade, shining all by itself deep in the ground with a stark unwholesome intensity that radiated from within its depths.

As the winch hauled the thing upward out of the hole, dragging it by a handle at one end, more of it came into sight.

He began to notice a series of inscriptions glinting along its edges. The coffin rotated slowly, catching the light, then settled into place as the makeshift crane set it down on the opposite side of the crater.

"Come on," Sam said.

Dean jogged behind him around the crater's outer rim. Several members of the Sheriff Daniels' investigation team had already gathered around the casket and were looking at it curiously. More were on their way over, along with one of the TV camera crews and a detachment of re-enactors who seemed to have become bolder about 'contaminating the crime scene.'

Hunching down in the middle of the group where he wouldn't be so conspicuous, Dean slipped his isolation hood off, letting the breeze cool the layer of sweat that had formed over his forehead and upper lip. He took in a deep breath and let it out. Either he'd actually started getting used to the smell of the pit, or it had begun to dissipate.

"Can you read any of this, Sam?" he asked.

Glancing around nervously, Sam took off his own mask for a better look and reached down to brush a remaining clod of dirt from the lid. The thing's surface shone out brightly, almost winking at them.

"It's familiar," he started. "These markings—" He stopped. "I think they match the symbols in Beauchamp's journal."

"This is Beauchamp's coffin, then."

"Yeah."

* * *

Before Sam could get a closer look, the group of workers that had brought out the coffin lifted it up and began carrying it back toward the waiting forensics vehicle. Following it into the open parking lot, Sam realized, would only leave him more exposed to the possibility of being recognized.

And then it was too late.

"Sam!"

He glanced up and saw what Dean had already noticed. On the other side of the pit, perhaps forty feet away, Sheriff Daniels was staring straight at him with a resolute expression that somehow combined recognition, determination, and anger. He supposed he'd known this would happen when he took off the hood... but some part of him hadn't expected that it would happen so fast.

"We're made," he said.

"Hang tight." Dean was backing up, glancing right and left. More than anything he resembled a quarterback taking stock of his options, even the utterly crazy ones. But they were out of time.

Daniels and her deputies were already moving toward them. There was no way out.

Damn it, Sam thought, *we're gonna spend the night in jail. Maybe more. And we don't have that kind of time.*

Suddenly Dean saw something that seemed to change the game for him. With a shout, he flung one hand up in the air.

"Yo, Commanches!"

Sam turned around and saw several state troopers escorting

a group of re-enactors that he identified as members of Dave Wolverton's division—the Fighting 32nd—past the still-panicked horses of the Confederate armed cavalry division. The soldier up in front was particularly familiar, and it took Sam less than five seconds to recognize Sarah Rafferty.

From where he stood, it looked like she was trying to get the horses out.

She looked up as Sheriff Daniels approached the Winchesters.

"Private Will Tanner!" Dean shouted. "Little help here?"

For an instant, Sarah didn't seem to understand what was being asked of her. Then she did.

The entire equation—the look on the sheriff's face, directed at Sam and Dean—unfolded in her expression, and she reached forward and grabbed the bolt on the horse paddock, opening the gate.

All the horses came spilling out in a great galloping wave. It was as if all the pent-up fear from the explosions had finally been given free rein. The animals cut across the open battleground in front of Sam and Dean, hooves thundering hard across the earth between the cops and emergency workers, forcing everyone backward with the atavistic dread that sends people scurrying out of the path of stampeding animals.

"Now!" Sam felt Dean's hand on his wrist. "Go!"

Using the stampede as cover, they yanked their masks back down and ran along behind the group of lab technicians carrying the casket toward the mobile crime lab. They helped load it into the back of the vehicle, then quickly climbed up after it. When they looked back down, the rest of the police forensics team—four of them, plus the driver—were climbing up into the back of the vehicle with them.

"Stay here," Dean said. "Me and my partner will handle this one."

"By yourselves?" The man in front took off his mask, his eyes flicking down to the badge around Dean's neck. "On whose orders?"

Before Dean could answer, there was a crash and a shout somewhere behind them. The horses were in the parking lot now, running between the cars and creating even more confusion.

The man in front whipped around to see what had happened.

"Let's move," Dean bellowed. He pulled the door shut and shouted back up to driver. "Where are we headed?"

"This is Federal jurisdiction now," the man behind the wheel called back. "We've got a plane waiting at Malcolm County Airport. Are you the only two riding along?"

"Looks that way," Sam said.

"Where's everybody else?"

Dean glanced out of the back window, where various members of state and local law enforcement had joined with the re-enactors in responding to the stampede.

"Rounding up horses. Looks like they stuck us with the stiff." He shrugged. "What are you gonna do?"

SEVENTEEN

The mobile crime scene truck rolled away from the battlefield and out of the parking lot, trundling down the country highway away from the town. It was bumpier than the road that led into town, and through the windows Sam saw the country landscape whipping past in a steady stream of green hills and blue sky.

"If those demons were taking the time to tear the whole field apart with cannon fire," Sam said, "they must have been pretty convinced that the noose was in Beauchamp's casket."

"So let's take a look."

Sam eyed the coffin.

"Now?" he said doubtfully. "You sure?"

"No problem. Find me a screwdriver."

"No, I mean, you really want to open this up?"

"That's why we're here, isn't it?"

"We don't even know what's going to happen."

Dean let out a breath.

"The coffin's pretty obviously not stopping the noose's power. So we need to get it out and destroy it."

"Just let me try Bobby first." Sam dug out his cell phone and dialed, waiting while it rang and finally went to voicemail. "He's not answering."

"That's it, then." Dean looked around. The back of the morgue vehicle was lined with steel cabinets and swing-bins of carefully stored instruments, chemical compounds, and medical tools. "Here." He picked up a shovel, and crouching beside the coffin wedged it underneath the lid. "This'll do."

The driver angled the rearview mirror, glowering back at them.

"Hey!" he shouted. "You know we aren't supposed to tamper with evidence."

"It's okay," Dean said. "We've got prior authorization."

"From who?"

"Uh, Colonel... Sanders."

"*What?*"

Sam shot his brother a glaring *WTF* stare. Dean just shrugged and twisted the shovel handle as hard as he could. Something inside the casket cracked wide open, and the hinges let out a low, creaking sound as the lid scraped upward.

"You guys aren't doing anything to that coffin, are you?"

Ignoring him, Dean levered the shovel down harder. Sam squatted next to him, hooking his fingers under the lid, flinching and catching his breath as he pried it upward.

"Whoa," Dean recoiled. "*More* stinky smell? Really?"

Sam shrugged and covered his nose. The back tires of the truck bumped upward, seeming to agitate the smell even more. It wasn't quite as rancid as the reek from the mass grave—but it was more intense, more preserved somehow, and spicy, like canned jerky that had been sequestered away somewhere for a century and a half.

Peering down, Sam looked into the casket's interior. It contained bones, most of them shifted to one side, where they looked smaller and somehow random. One of the ribs was tangled in what looked like an old suspender, complete with a metal buckle. There was a rusty old revolver that had long ago started reverting into its component parts.

"Oh, man. What happened?" Dean poked through the rest of their stained and brittle remains, looking like a kid whose Christmas toy had arrived broken before he'd gotten a chance to play with it. He picked up the toppled-loose skull and set it aside.

Shards of human pottery and a pair of broken-down hobnailed boots were all that remained of Jubal Beauchamp. There were tattered gray rags of his uniform and a few brass buttons rattling around the bottom like loose teeth, and that was all.

"Talk about no prize in the Crackerjacks," Dean said. "Where's the noose?"

"It's not here."

"Hey!" the driver was looking back at them. "*Hey!*"

"Well, where is it then?"

"I don't know, Dean."

"Why don't we ask Johnny Reb here." Dean picked up Beauchamp's skull again and turned it around to face him, Hamlet-style. "Hey, Jubal. Where's the noose, huh, buddy?" He turned to Sam. "What do you know, he ain't talking either."

"Dean—"

But Dean wasn't looking at him anymore. He was staring directly at the skull, still in his hand, at the thin dark tendrils of smoky-colored substance that had begun to drift out of its empty sockets.

"Uh, Dean...?"

The black substance began to float upward, still sluggish, as if awakened from a long sleep. There was something swirling in its depths, Sam realized, something alive and hideously aware.

Moa'ah.

The stuff floating in front of him swirled around Sam's head with slow, exploratory curiosity, forming a ring that, under the circumstances, reminded him of a noose. It reminded him of the way squid-ink moved through water... except that it was drifting through the air, hanging suspended in the back of the truck.

For a second it appeared to hook around in the shape of a question mark. Then it tightened.

Sam's head began to throb, as if they'd just gone through an abrupt change in barometric pressure. He felt dizzy, sick to his stomach, like a man who's just realized he's coming down with a particularly nasty strain of the flu.

"Don't look at it," Dean said.

"Don't...?" Sam arched an eyebrow. "Is this a *Raiders of the Lost Ark* thing?"

"Damn it, Sam—"

"Okay, all right, I'm not looking."

"And no sudden moves," Dean said. "I think it's still waking up. It's been locked in the dark for a long time." His eyes darted, following the motion of the thing in the air. "But pretty soon it's going to realize it's been messed with and get pissed.

"I'm going to put the skull down," he added.

"Good idea."

As gently as possible, he set it back into the coffin. The Moa'ah that had emerged from the eye-sockets began slithering back down, pouring itself inside. It was as if, given the choice of attacking a stranger or staying with the human remains that had been its companion for the last hundred and sixty years, it had chosen the familiar option.

At least for now.

"What in God's name...?" the driver bawled from up in front. He turned around to peer angrily into the back. "The whole truck stinks to high heaven!"

"Sorry." Dean's voice was a shaky attempt at normalcy. "Army beans for breakfast."

"You can't—"

"Look out!" Sam shouted.

The driver looked back around, but it was too late. The station wagon that was parked up ahead of them, directly across the double-yellow line, was less than twenty feet away when he hit the brakes. The forensics van was still going sixty miles an hour when it slammed into it broadside, T-boning it with the full impact of its one and a half tons of steel.

For an instant the whole world went red. Then, one by one, Sam's senses began returning.

He heard glass shattering, and he and Dean were pitched forward with the force of impact, bouncing off the metal cabinets and canisters of supplies.

A jar of foul-smelling fluid burst open underneath him, filling the air with the acrid spirits of formaldehyde. The coffin full of bones flew forward too, a prisoner of its own velocity. Thrown by the momentum, the open iron box shot straight ahead as if fired by some invisible slingshot, smashing straight up into the driver's seat, and there was a third burst of glass as the van's windshield gave way.

Up in the cab, the driver started to scream. Vaguely, like images glimpsed through a foggy windowpane, Sam saw the black substance enveloping the man's head. It did something to his face. He thrashed violently in his seatbelt, arms hooking the air, fighting to get loose.

Then the screaming stopped.

In the silence that followed, Sam became aware of a squelching, sucking sound coming from the front of the van, from where the driver was sitting. The Moa'ah was still up there, he realized, still wrapped around the driver's face. Absurdly, his mind gibbered with an immortal line from 'A Visit from Saint Nicholas.'

It encircled his head like a wreath.

There was a tinkling of broken glass and spilled tools behind him as Dean lifted himself up from the floor of the van with a groan.

"Sammy? You all right?"

"Yeah." Except he wasn't. His shoulder ached, and his right hip felt as if someone had gone to work on it with a sledgehammer. Nevertheless, he picked himself up out of the rubble. "I'm going to go up and check on the driver."

Limping a little, he ducked down and crept his way forward toward the front seat. For a moment his attention was completely arrested by the view through the smashed-in windshield. The van had knocked the station wagon completely off the highway, throwing it sideways into a ditch on the far right side of the road where it lay, half-accordioned, the hood hissing steam. The entire wood-paneled side had been punched in, but Sam could see that it was empty. Whoever had parked it lengthwise across the double yellow line had simply abandoned it there.

He shifted his attention. Directly in front of the van, not far from the grille, Beauchamp's coffin lay in the middle of the road where the impact of the collision had flung it. The coffin had landed sideways and Sam saw Beauchamp's bones strewn out across the asphalt. Only a cluster of them remained in the coffin.

He couldn't see the skull, but it had to be out there somewhere. The other bones looked like pieces from some extravagantly complex dice game whose results determined the cosmic fate of all parties involved.

Finally, he glanced sideways at the driver's seat. He could see the back of the driver's head, angled slightly to the left as if the man were checking his side-view mirror.

"Hey, buddy." He didn't really expect an answer.

Taking one last step forward—so that he was in line with the driver and passenger seats—Sam tapped the man's shoulder, then shook it. The head lolled around to reveal a gaping red hole where his face should have been. The driver's eyes, nose and mouth had been scooped out, all the way back to the occipital region of his skull. The front of his shirt was a bib of gore, gray brain matter and windshield glass.

Sam's mind flashed to the man's screams, and the sucking sounds that followed.

The Moa'ah did this to him. But why?

Then he saw it.

Beauchamp's skull had fallen out of the coffin during its brief, violent trip forward.

And it had landed on the driver's lap.

He looked closer. Hovering just inside the eye sockets, on the brink of visibility, was the pulsating black substance.

It might not have been fully awake before, Sam thought, *but it's awake now. And Dean was right: it* is *pissed.*

"Sam?" Dean's voice called from the back. "How bad is it up there?"

Sam didn't answer. He scarcely breathed.

Gingerly, like a man picking up a nest of swarming

hornets, he made himself lift Beauchamp's skull, gripping it from the back. He could feel the Moa'ah humming around inside, filling its hollow bony hemisphere, like a cell phone set on vibrate. He held the skull briefly in his fingertips, then turned and hurled it as hard as fast as he could through the hole in the blown-out windshield out onto the road in front of them. It clattered once and rolled across the pavement, coming to rest next to a black boot.

"Thank you, Sam. How considerate of you to do our work for us."

Sam looked up at the source of the sardonic voice.

Perhaps twenty yards ahead, a group of five re-enactors in Union and Confederate uniforms and hats were standing shoulder to shoulder in the middle of the road. They smiled, and their eyes flicked jet-black.

"Dean," Sam felt a surge of exhaustion, "demons."

"I'll alert the media," Dean muttered.

"Sam and Dean Winchester," the Confederate soldier next to the skull said, "again we prove that there's nothing you can possess we cannot take away."

Dean groaned.

"Is he quoting *Raiders*?"

"It seemed appropriate," the demon said. "Nice hazmat suits, by the way. Got tired of the FBI outfits, did you?"

Without waiting for a response, the demon bent down and picked up Beauchamp's skull, holding it at arm's length to better investigate the Moa'ah pulsating inside it.

"Where's the noose, boys?" he asked.

"It's not there," Dean said.

"What?"

"You heard me, ugly." Dean had squeezed past Sam now and into the passenger seat, opening the door and climbing out. "Looks like you fellas got hold of some false intel."

"Don't bother lying to us."

"We're not," Sam said. "The noose wasn't in the coffin. See for yourself."

Still holding Beauchamp's skull in one hand, the soldier demon moved forward toward the casket, the others following behind. Two of them squatted down, searching through the bones and debris.

"He's right," one of them confirmed. "It's not here."

"Looks like you just bit the bag and stepped out the door, sunshine," Dean said. "Don't say we didn't—"

The Confederate soldier roared a snarl of furious rage. Then he threw the skull down as hard as he could. It cracked, but didn't shatter.

"I wouldn't do that," Sam said, climbing out next to his brother.

Ignoring him, the demon brought a boot down on the skull—hard.

Two things happened at once.

The skull broke open under his heel with a brisk ceramic crack, and the Moa'ah—in its full awakened and angry state—came spurting up and outward, rounding in midair and plunging back toward the demon with a violent spearlike thrust.

Sam had never heard a demon scream quite like it. The Moa'ah eviscerated its meat-suit in less than a second, ripping directly through the Confederate soldier's chest cavity and almost splitting it in two.

The demon shrieked and flashed out, but before its parts even hit the asphalt, the Moa'ah had changed course again, arcing back on the other demons gathered around Beauchamp's bones. It tore through demons two and three with a speed and fury that was almost too fast to see, and flashed around to wipe out the last two with a single slashing downward stroke.

Then it swirled back around, settling among dissolute bones in the coffin that had been its home for the past century and a half. The lid swung shut with a clank.

"Whoa," Dean said. "Should we run now?"

"Yeah. Running's good."

"So," Dean said. "How far do you think it is back to town?"

"Couple miles."

"Great."

Sam glanced at him.

"What?"

"'Cuz, you know," Dean patted his flat stomach, "I could really use the exercise."

They both spun around and broke into a sprint.

They hadn't gone twenty feet when they saw the police lights careening straight up the road at them from the direction of town, coming too fast to dodge.

EIGHTEEN

The cruiser's tires scraped to a halt in front of them and Sheriff Daniels sprang out of the car, handcuffs already in hand. The ferocity of her expression alone would have smelted steel.

"You two have no idea how much trouble you're in," she said. "You're both—"

"Under arrest," Dean finished. "Yeah, we get it."

"Up against the car." Jamming Sam forward, Daniels jerked his hands back and clapped the metal bracelets on his wrists, frisking him thoroughly. "Spread your legs."

"Hey," Dean said, "don't forget me."

Daniels stuffed Sam into the back seat of the cruiser. From the passenger seat, her big swag-bellied deputy—*Jerry* was the name that Dean fished out of his memory—stepped out, ready with the sap should things turn ugly. At first Dean thought the guy was going to be the one to frisk him, proving yet again that his bad luck was coming in streaks. But then the deputy saw the wreckage of the truck in the road ahead and kept walking.

"Hey, sheriff," he shouted back. "You're gonna want to check this out."

"Hold on." Daniels quickly cuffed Dean, and he felt her hands go over his body, patting him down roughly.

"Whoa," Dean said. "Try a little tenderness, huh?"

"What's this?" She yanked out Ruby's demon-killing knife and examined it.

"I'm going to need that back."

"I don't think so." She opened the back of the cruiser and shoved him in next to Sam, slamming the door behind them. It was cramped and smelled like some generic bleach-based disinfectant. With his hands cuffed behind him, Dean had to lean forward, bent over his knees. There were two door handles on the inside back doors, and the wire mesh separating them from the front was caged steel.

"Well, this sucks," he observed.

Sam nodded and watched Sheriff Daniels walking up the road to join the deputy. Suddenly he heard Jerry's voice.

"Holy crap!"

"Sounds like they found the meat-suits," Dean said.

"Yup."

"They'll pin it all on us, y'know."

"No doubt."

They watched as Sheriff Daniels spun and headed back toward the cruiser, walking fast, almost running. She slid into the front seat and picked up her radio, keying the mic.

"This is Sheriff Daniels requesting immediate backup at a single-vehicle MVA on Highway 17, mile-marker 83. Multiple confirmed casualties, red-blanket, notify emergency services."

The radio crackled and an ambulance dispatcher confirmed the request, echoing it back.

"I hope you two have good lawyers," Daniels said, glaring at them in the rearview mirror. "You're going to need them."

"We have some people we can call," Dean said.

The sheriff didn't reply. As she turned the microphone around and put it back, her sleeve rose up slightly, and Dean noticed something he'd never seen before—a small symbolic tattoo spread over her right wrist. It was a ring of numbers, surrounded by a tiny ring of stars. Inside the smaller circle, two overlapping pentagrams formed an oddly asymmetrical design, like a kind of web.

He snapped a glance at Sam, who nodded back at him. He'd seen it, too.

"Nice ink," Dean said.

Daniels stiffened. Without looking back, she tugged the shirt-cuff down again over the design, covering it up.

"I'm taking you back to the station," she said. "My deputy's waiting here for backup."

"That's a Santeria charm, isn't it?" Sam asked.

The sheriff started the engine and swung the car around. She gunned it, the cruiser's big V-8 roaring as the landscape around them became an afterthought.

"How much do you really know about that noose?"

Sam asked. "What are you using it for?"

Daniels' face flashed from the rearview mirror.

"If I were you, I'd keep quiet until I had counsel present."

"You've got bigger problems than us, lady," Dean said. "You saw the driver. You think *we* did that to him?" He shook his head. "There's stuff walking around in those woods out there that you don't even have names for."

The sheriff glanced back.

"You'd be surprised—" she began, and in front of them, fifty yards ahead, something burst out of the woods and went streaking into the road. At first, out of sheer surprise, Dean thought it was an animal, maybe a deer. Then he realized it was a man standing on the broken yellow line staring back at them with a kind of distant intensity that Dean associated with just one individual in his life.

"Look out!" he shouted.

Up ahead, Castiel didn't budge. Daniels jerked her head forward, saw him standing there and slammed on the brakes. The cruiser slung around sideways, skidding and fishtailing across both lanes and over the shoulder, rolling onto its side and down into the gully.

Second crash of the day, Dean thought through the haze. *Good deal.*

In the front seat, Daniels was bent over sideways, still conscious, struggling to get out of her seatbelt.

Outside, Castiel sprang past the driver's side door and jerked open the back, grabbing Dean and hauling him out, then reaching in for Sam.

The sheriff squirmed around.

"Who the hell are you?"

"Run." Castiel looked winded, as if what he'd just done had taxed him to the limit. "*Go.*"

Sam and Dean scrambled over the shoulder and down the embankment, crashing into the woods with their hands still cuffed behind them. The sun blazed down, flashing through the leaves. Every direction looked the same. They ran deeper into the woods, already lost and disoriented, until Dean realized there was no chance of finding their way back out again.

They kept going, moving forward for half an hour. Incredibly, the foliage around them grew thicker still. Branches clutched and grabbed at their clothing, as if the landscape itself had turned against them. Neither of them spoke.

The uneven terrain was marred by fallen branches, tangled brambles, and holes in the ground, and Sam knew that if he or Dean stepped into one and twisted an ankle, they'd be done for. There was no way one of them could carry the other with their hands cuffed behind them.

What happens if it's you, Sam? a voice asked. It was the voice from his dream. *Would you leave your brother behind?*

No, of course not, Sam replied silently.

Oh really? Thirty silver pieces say otherwise.

Sam pushed the thought out of his head. It wasn't difficult. He forced himself to concentrate on moving forward, forward, forward.

Then they hit the swamp.

"Stop," Dean gasped. "You hear that?"

Sam shook his head. They'd been running hard and the only thing he could hear was his own heart pounding and his breath tea-kettling in and out of his lungs. His chest was on fire, the flames shooting up his throat into his head.

"*Listen.*"

"Dean..."

"Shh!"

Sam staggered around sideways, sweat dripping from his face. They were standing in a thicket of vines and root systems, amid swarms of buzzing mosquitoes that hovered over his face in clouds, filling his ears with their constant whine. His damp wrists squirmed in the cuffs, his hands begging illogically to wave the bugs away. Mossy fungus smells rose up from the ground. His legs were soaked to the knees with thick black muck that seemed to suck and clutch at the fabric of his pants with every laborious step.

He waited, listening.

And then he heard it.

Barking. Yelping.

Baying.

"Are those *bloodhounds?*"

Dean didn't answer. He was facing in the opposite direction. When Sam finally caught a look at his brother's face, he saw that Dean's cheeks and forehead had gone absolutely white, as if every drop of blood had been sucked away, leaving his complexion frightened and hollow. The result made his eyes burn so feverishly green that they were almost incandescent.

"Dean—"

"We gotta run." Dean was trembling so hard that his voice was shaking. His eyes were twitching everywhere at once. "We gotta outrun them, Sammy."

"They're not hellhounds, Dean. They're just dogs."

"They're on our trail!"

"Okay, look," Sam stalked a few steps forward, felt the muck growing steadily softer under his boots, "it's swampy through here. Which means we're near a creek. If we can get through it, they'll lose our scent. Right?"

Dean didn't answer. He was still listening to the barking and howling noises coming closer, crashing through the undergrowth. He seemed paralyzed by the sounds.

No more time. If we're going to do something, do it now.

Sam threw his shoulder against his brother and knocked him forward, forcing Dean to go stomping along next to him. The smell of the swamp filled his nose, a rich, fungal scent of dead logs and stagnant water, coming from straight ahead of them. Deep puddles splashed around them, reeds and cattails rustling up ahead in strange whispering sighs. Frogs croaked. He felt the water, sun-warmed at the surface but cold and viscous below, surging up to his knees, and then, abruptly, his waist.

After a momentary pause, Sam just grunted and kept going, glancing over at his brother from time to time. But

Dean was moving on his own now.

It was getting more difficult to drag his boots up from the bottom. The hounds sounded very close, near enough that if he turned around, he thought he might actually see the foliage moving behind them. Exhaustion had taken hold of his muscles and wrung them out.

They made their way through lily pads and pond scum, heads tilted back as the water went up to their necks.

"Sam?" Dean's whisper sounded uneven and high. "Not getting any shallower here."

Sam nodded and took another step. Suddenly the muddy bottom was gone and he went under. His feet hit something on the bottom, and he pushed upward. Shooting back to the surface with a gasp, spluttering and spitting out dirty water, he felt something slide past his calf. A water moccasin curved its way across the surface and slashed into the high grass.

He let out a sharp breath, a switchblade of panic flipping open in his stomach. He lunged forward, and found purchase for his feet again, thrashing along blindly with no regard for speed, direction or the noise he was making, unaware even of how much time had passed until Dean hissed his name from somewhere behind him.

"*Wait*," Dean said. "Don't move."

Sam fell still. The veil of flying insect bites tightened around his scalp and neck. Every inch of his skin seemed to crawl. He was aware of his own breath rippling over the water in front of his face.

"They're going the other way."

It was true—the howling, hooting noises of the dogs were dopplering away from them now, receding into the distance, deeper into the woods.

"Lost 'em," Dean breathed, then he sniffed the air, his voice different now. "Wait a minute. Do you smell smoke?"

"Yeah." Sam looked and caught a glimpse of orange flame flickering through the trees. "It's coming from over there."

Moving cautiously, they pulled themselves out of the water. Then they made their way into a small clearing.

A campfire burned unattended.

Two Civil War tents, neither of them any more sophisticated than the makeshift canvas-and-rope contraptions they'd seen back on the battlefield, leaned against a copse of scrub oak on the far edge of the swamp. In the fire-pit, the flames were burning down, and the last embers smoldered, keeping the bugs at bay. Scraps of wool uniforms, abandoned breeches, knapsacks and boots, all lay scattered on the periphery, where their wearers seemed to have cast them off without regard to where they'd fallen.

Some of them appeared to have been ripped off.

"Dean?"

Dean sniffed.

"Yeah, that's sulfur."

"Okay, demons." Sam poked the fire with his toe. There were cans of lighter fluid next to it. "Meaning what?"

"We shouldn't stay and roast marshmallows?"

"We should check the tents."

Dean gave him a look.

"Really?"

"Maybe there're some tools we can use to get these cuffs off."

"Yeah. Meanwhile, if there's anything bigger than a bumblebee in there, it's going to kick our ass."

"There's nobody here."

Dean walked over and kicked open the flap in front of him, leaning down.

"You're right," he said. "Just a few candy wrappers. Man, these demons are total slobs. Yours?"

Sam squatted down and looked into his tent. At first he thought the lump in the shadows was just a dirty bedroll with more torn clothing strewn over it. Then he heard the flies droning around it with their meaningless little fly noises. Sliding one foot in, he kicked off the stained Confederate flag draped over the pile.

It wasn't a bedroll.

The bloated corpse of the man under the flag seemed to grin up at him. He was stripped to the waist with his arms and legs tied down with ropes and staked directly into the ground. Hooks pierced his lips, cheeks and eyelids, and wires pulled them back. The flesh of his chest and belly had been peeled away, layer by layer, exposing red muscle and tissue beneath it, a life-sized anatomy lesson.

In the center of his chest, a larger iron hook on a heavier chain plunged through the open rib cage, impaling his heart.

"Holy crap," Dean said, peering over Sam's shoulder. "It's Winston."

"Who?"

"The coroner, Todd Winston. The sheriff's brother-in-law."

"They tortured him."

"Demons don't normally do this. They torture souls in Hell, but..." Dean shook his head, stepping into the tent. "They must have really wanted to get some information from him, and badly."

He leaned forward, toeing a rag-wrapped bundle next to Winston's head, and Sam heard metal instruments clinking together.

"Sounds like some medieval stuff in here."

"Like what?"

Dean didn't answer. He was gazing down at what he'd uncovered. The tool at his feet looked like an oversized pair of pliers combined with the blades of a bone saw, their serrated edges caked with untold decades of dried blood, clots of hair and human grease.

"You know how to use those?" Sam asked.

"Yeah," Dean said evenly. "I do."

Backing up next to Winston's staked-out corpse, he sank down to his knees, clutching the tool behind his back. For a moment he maneuvered his shoulders and elbows around and then Sam heard the chain break open with a sharp, brittle clank.

Dean's hands appeared in front of him again, a steel

bracelet on each wrist.

"Got it," he said. "Now you."

He lifted the sharpened pliers again and snapped the chain on Sam's cuffs.

"Thanks."

"Don't mention it."

Dean emerged from the tent and looked down at the campfire. He bent down and picked up a can of lighter fluid in both hands, then started spraying it over the ground as he moved back toward the tent.

"Stand back."

"Hang on. I'm going to take another look at Winston's corpse first."

"What? Why?"

"I think I saw something on his wrist." Drawing aside the flap, Sam ducked back into the tent and bent down beside the corpse, inspecting its arm.

"Hey, Dean?"

"Yeah?"

"Check this out." Sam pointed to Winston's left wrist. The skin was blistered and scorched black, as if someone had endeavored to burn it off, but he could still make out the tattoo imprinted there. "That's another Santeria sigil, isn't it?"

"Like the one Sheriff Daniels had, yeah," Dean said. "What's it mean?"

"Demons wanted it off."

"Or somebody did." Dean held up the lighter fluid. "We finished here?"

Sam nodded, and Dean tossed him a can of his own. They

sprayed the tent along with the demons' clothes and supplies, and when they were finished, Dean picked up a glowing log from the fire and tossed it.

"Good riddance," he muttered as they turned and walked away.

They picked a direction and started walking, slashing their way back through the brush and undergrowth. It was easier going with their hands free—or at least easier to wave away the mosquitoes—but Sam still had no real sense of direction. The demon camp had sent his inner compass-needle spinning recklessly out of control, as if they'd stumbled across some disorienting magnetic field.

"It's getting marshy again," Dean said, cutting through another puddle of water. "We're not walking in circles, are we?"

"I don't know."

"Great." With a groan, Dean reached into his back pocket and pulled out his cell phone, poking listlessly at the buttons. "Thing's ruined. I knew it would be. You got yours?"

"Nope. It's a dud, too."

Dean frowned.

"Wait a second, what the hell's *that*?"

Sam squinted across the clearing up ahead where the last vines and branches gave way to a parking lot.

"Is that..." Dean shielded his eyes, "...a Walmart?"

They waded up out of the water, past an upended shopping cart and stood there, dripping and filthy, in the late afternoon heat. For a moment neither of them spoke.

From where they stood, alongside the outer border of the swamp, the store gleamed in the distance, city-sized, *planet*-sized. Out here in the hinterlands of its parking lot, most of the spaces were empty except for a couple of RVs and eighteen-wheelers that looked as if they'd come to rest months ago. The closest one was a Winnebago the size of a city bus with a satellite dish and an airbrushed mural of wild horses running across a desert. It could have belonged to a pair of 401K-savvy retirees, or Kid Rock's backup band.

"I guess we probably can't just go up and ask for a ride," Sam offered.

"No," Dean said, then brightened. "But I bet there's a pay phone in the store."

Sam looked at his brother in the torn hazmat suit, tattered and covered with mud, and said nothing.

NINETEEN

It was nearing dusk when the black Ford Ranger swung up in front of the Walmart tire and automotive center and flashed its headlights.

Dean and Sam ran over and jumped into the cargo bed. Climbing in, Dean was vaguely reassured to see that the pickup was equipped with a fully supplied gun-rack. There was a modern pump-action shotgun resting on top, and below it, a perfectly tooled Civil War musket that looked just as lethal. Underneath that, behind the seat, was a canister of road salt.

"Rufus wouldn't let me leave home without it," Tommy McClane said, peering into the back and noticing Dean's eyes on the weapon.

"Good for him."

"I'd offer you a ride up front, but you two look like you've been mud-wrestling with a catfish." He blinked in genuine amazement. "Are those hazmat suits?"

"Something like that," Dean said.

"Should I even ask?"

"We'll tell you everything when we get the chance. Right now I just want to get out of here."

"Just lay low, stay under the tarp. Sheriff's got roadblocks up, but it's getting dark. I think I can get you through 'em."

Dean pulled the roll of canvas over them and felt the pickup pull forward and curve around the lot. Soon the country highway was humming along underneath them. Dean shut his eyes. He was exhausted and wanted a shower, a burger, and a beer.

Huddled next to him, Sam wasn't saying anything, and that was fine with him. He had more than enough on his mind already.

Those pliers, for example, back at the camp.

He hadn't seen those since Hell.

And in Hell, he'd used them every day.

Stop. You're not up for this now.

He straightened up a little, and then tensed. The truck was slowing down, and then stopped. He heard voices and footsteps outside. A cop's flashlight moved over the outside of the tarp.

"What do you have underneath there?" the cop's voice asked.

"Table and chairs," Tommy replied. He sounded slow and laconic, almost bored. "Promised my ex that I'd refinish 'em for her. Amazing what a man'll do for a six-pack and a little nostalgia sex, you know what I mean?" The truck door swung open as Tommy stepped down. "Here, I'll show you."

Come on, man, Dean thought, too tired even to worry about it. *We aren't the droids you're looking for.*

"Yeah, show a little consideration, and she gets all misty eyed," Tommy continued. "Last time I did some chores for her, she just stripped down, right there in the living room, and—"

"Now hold on a second," the cop said. He sounded upset.

"Yes, officer?"

"Do I look like someone who cares about your sex life? That's entirely too much information. Why don't you just haul your ass outta here, and stop wasting my time."

"Suit yourself." The pickup lurched a little again, the door slamming shut, the flashlight waving.

"Move along," the cop said, "and drive safely."

Back at the McClanes' house, Sam and Dean found almost everything they wanted—hydrocortisone cream for Sam's mosquito bites and, best of all, fresh hot cheeseburgers from Tommy's kitchen stove.

They washed them down with cold beer while Nate brought a pair of bolt-cutters from the garage and cut the cuffs off, after which they spent twenty minutes rubbing the raw-red bruises encircling their wrists.

Sam finished eating and then used Tommy's land-line to call Sarah Rafferty's cell phone. She answered on the second ring, sounding glad to hear from them.

"After what happened out on the battlefield today," she said, "I was worried about you both."

"It would have been a lot worse if it weren't for you," Sam told her. "That was quick thinking."

"I just remembered what you said about the sheriff. How she was more hindrance than help. But Sam..." Sarah's voice hesitated a little, "are you really with the FBI?"

"No," he said. "It's something else."

"What is it? Another government agency?"

"Not exactly. I don't think it would make much sense if I tried to explain it."

"You might be surprised," she said. "But I won't press you. Not if you're really trying to figure out what happened with Dave.

"That is what you're doing, isn't it?" she added.

"Yes. That hasn't changed."

"Then I'm glad I helped you." She sighed, and it was a shaky, restless sound. "At least I think so."

"Where are you, Sarah?"

"I'm still out by the battleground. A lot of us are, actually—the re-enactors, I mean. The police have stopped trying to drive us off, for now anyway. They haven't even had a chance to get those howitzers off the cliffside yet. We told them we're not going anywhere until we get a reasonable explanation of what happened out there today, and so far, the authorities haven't even acknowledged that anything out of the ordinary happened at all. It's like Sheriff Daniels sneezed, and they all caught the misinformation flu."

The misinformation flu. Sam found it an oddly apt turn of phrase. "Just be careful," he said. "Take care of yourself.

We'll talk to you soon."

"And you'll explain more?"

"I'll try," he said. It was the closest he could come to the truth, and hoped for now it would be enough.

When Dean finished his beer, he pushed back his plate and stood up, turning to face Tommy.

"I don't suppose there's any way we could clean up a little."

"I was wondering when we'd get around to that." Tommy eyed the tattered hazmat suits that the Winchesters were still wearing. "I'd offer some of my gear, but you're both taller than me and I don't have clean clothes either one of you could fit into."

"Our stuff is back at the motel," Sam said. "At this point we can't very well go back and get it ourselves."

"Yeah, the cops'll be watching it," Tommy agreed. He glanced around, one eyebrow cocked. "There's a general store in town where I could go pick up some clean clothes for you—jeans and t-shirts, at least. Y'all could just hang out here with Nate."

"Much appreciated," Sam said. He opened his wallet and handed Tommy some cash for the clothes. "I'll even finish the dishes."

"That's a deal."

Tommy paused as if to consider something.

"Oh, and Sam?"

"What?"

"Don't get me wrong, I'm on your side—you're hunters,

after all. But when I get back, and you are all showered and clean—" He looked straight at Sam, his expression grim. "I'd appreciate an explanation of just what the hell is going on here."

"Don't worry, you'll get it."

Tommy turned and left, and Sam took his place at the sink and began washing the plates and cutlery. A moment later Nate came up alongside him and began wiping them dry before placing them carefully on the drying rack. The boy worked quickly, with easy efficiency. Glancing over at him, Sam noticed the automatic Whirlpool unit installed alongside the kitchen sink.

"You've got a dishwasher," Sam said. "Don't you use it?"

Nate shrugged.

"It's just the two of us here. Dad says it's not worth running."

"Right." Sam handed him another dish, and the boy dried it, front and back, with a couple deft swipes of the hand-towel.

Balanced on the shelf in front of them was a photo in a simple wooden frame, Tommy McClane and a pretty twenty-something redhead in a pale pink scoop-neck blouse and jade earrings, holding a toddler. The toddler—obviously a one year-old Nate—was wearing a giant, crooked grin and a t-shirt reading: I DO ALL MY OWN STUNTS.

"My brother and I grew up without a mom, too," Sam said. He passed Nate another dish, and the boy took it without comment, rinsed and wiped and racked it. "It wasn't always easy." That was the last of the plates, and he turned the water off and wiped his hands on a towel. "Not everybody gets that."

The boy still didn't say anything, or even look up, and for a second Sam thought he'd overstepped his boundaries, become too personal. But then Nate did look up, his face uncertain, almost puzzled.

"Did you like your dad?" he asked.

"My dad..." Sam started, unsure how to proceed, "taught me a lot. He tried."

"Mine too," Nate said. "The stuff he talks about, it freaks me out sometimes, you know? I think he wants me to be like him when I grow up, take over the Historical Society and... everything else. But sometimes..." He shrugged.

"What?"

"My mom was an artist. I mean, what if I decide to do that instead?"

"Then you should," Sam told him. "If that's what you want to do, you should follow it."

Nate frowned again.

"I still dream about her sometimes, you know? Even though I was so young when she... when it happened." He blinked at Sam. "Weird, huh?"

"Are they good dreams?"

"Yeah."

"Then it's good. That's your way of remembering her."

Not long after, the front door opened and Tommy came back with new clothes. Sam and Dean went upstairs to take turns showering and getting changed.

As he washed off the dirt and grime of the day, Sam made a mental note to ask the boy more about his mother.

After Dean and Sam got cleaned up, they all sat back down in the big old-fashioned plantation kitchen, gathered around McClane's pine table. The windows were open and the night-sounds of crickets and cicadas rippled in through the screens. Far off in the distance, lightning pulsed and flickered in the darkness, followed by the distant rumble of thunder.

Tommy had the Braves game playing softly on the radio and the reception blurred into static as the storm moved closer.

"All right," he said finally. "I've waited long enough. You gonna tell me what happened to you out there?"

Dean cracked a fresh beer while Sam told Tommy and Nate about what they'd seen on the road, the floating black substance that had come oozing from Beauchamp's remains, and how Dean had seen the same thing coming out of Dave Wolverton's corpse.

When Sam finished, Tommy nodded slowly.

"So the thing about the Moa'ah," he began, "is it's the animating force behind the noose, but its presence doesn't always mean the noose is still nearby. Hell, it can hover around the infected, sometimes for decades, even centuries, until it gets a chance to air out."

"I guess nobody told the demons that," Sam said.

"Or they're just that desperate." Tommy ran one hand thoughtfully over the wood-grain of the table. "If the demons were torturing civilians for information, like you said, that sounds pretty desperate."

"What about Sheriff Daniels?" Dean asked. "For that matter, what about my car? And our knife?"

Tommy nodded.

"The knife and the car, I can probably help you with," he said. "But Jacqueline Daniels isn't a woman you want to mess with."

"We saw her Santeria tattoo."

"That's the least of it. Her family goes back to the original battle of Mission's Ridge." Tommy's voice darkened a little, and he glanced over at Nate, who had been sitting in silence at the end of the table, listening intently. "Why don't you run upstairs and get ready for bed."

"Do I have to?"

Tommy shot him a stern look.

"You heard me."

The boy sulked off, mumbling under his breath, and when his footsteps faded up the stairs, Tommy sat back and opened a little drawer in the table, taking out a pack of American Spirits and a lighter.

He glanced up at the Winchesters a little sheepishly.

"You mind? I've cut down to one a day, but if I'm going to tell you this story, I think I'm gonna need it."

He shook out a cigarette and lit it, inhaled, then sat back and blew a stream of smoke toward the window.

"You said you saw that tattoo on her wrist. That's not actually Santeria in the traditional sense. For generations now, the Daniels family has been practicing their own twisted version of backwoods witchcraft. It started with her great-great-great-great grandfather, who came up from the Louisiana bayou back before the war and set up shop outside of Mission's Ridge. Not long after that, local people started disappearing."

"That was Daniels' ancestor?"

Tommy nodded. "He started abducting people, slaves and children mainly, to experiment on them. There were rumors of human sacrifice, cannibalism, and vivisection using human subjects while they were still alive and conscious. Daniels was trying out some of the... variations on African rituals he'd learned back in New Orleans."

He dragged on the cigarette again. It was almost halfway gone already.

The kitchen felt darker now.

"After a year or so," he continued, "some of the locals got together and lynched him for it. Hung him up and burned him alive. It's all in the public record, if you care to dig a little. On the night he died, his infant son was whisked away and raised by another family. He grew up to be a Civil War doctor named..."

"My God." McClane scraped back his chair and stood up. For the first time he actually looked shaken. "Aristede Percy," he looked at Sam, "you said when you were reading Beauchamp's journal that he was the Civil War doctor who supposedly used the powers of the noose to bring Jubal back to life."

McClane sank back into his chair, his face alive with the possibilities the connection opened up.

"Tomorrow marks the two hundred-year anniversary of Daniels' lynching," he added. He opened the pack of cigarettes again, considered it briefly then put it away. "The noose's power will most probably be at its peak. We've already seen its effects, even though the actual rope has yet to be recovered."

"It's out there somewhere, though," Sam said.

McClane nodded. His face was a grim mask.

"And Jacqueline Daniels won't rest until she finds it."

"She's the sheriff," Sam said. "How do we stop her?"

"You have to get to it first. Use a special weapon and cut the thing to pieces."

"Like a supernatural weapon." Dean half-laughed, then looked glum. "We had one of those once."

"You mean this?"

McClane reached into a leather sheath on his belt and took out Ruby's demon-killing knife, sliding it across the table to Dean. The sight of it made Dean's face light up with such enthusiasm that he almost looked childlike.

"Where'd you get that?"

"Let's just say I've got a few connections in the sheriff's office. Stuff disappears from the evidence cage all the time. Thankfully, Sheriff Daniels doesn't have any idea what this particular item is capable of. If she did..." McClane shuddered, letting the thought drift away unarticulated.

"So we've got the knife back," Dean said, his mood

darkening again. "What about the Impala?"

"In the impound lot. We can see about getting it in the morning. I'll talk to Raymond Ungeroot—he's one of the deputies down there. Also my nephew." Dean tossed him a look, and Tommy looked a little chagrined. "What can I say, it's a real small town."

"Any idea where the noose is?" Dean asked.

"On that score," McClane said, shaking his head, "I got nothing."

"No," Sam said, "but I might. We're going to need a ride into town."

TWENTY

The old church was silent.

Sam and Dean approached the front steps, both holding flashlights that Tommy McClane had supplied.

Somewhere in the distance a dog yapped twice, howled and fell quiet. It was two a.m., and the narrow side streets of the town had lapsed into a thick, narcoleptic stillness that was as close to slumber as it was going to get.

"First Pentecostal Church of Mission's Ridge," Dean read, and then he turned to Sam.

Sam shone his flashlight on the cornerstone, looking at the date.

"Year of Our Lord 1833. It's the oldest remaining building in town. The one structure the Union army didn't torch after General Meade whipped the Rebels out on the hill." He gestured around the side. "And according to what Sarah Rafferty told us, this is where it all changed for Dave

Wolverton—on Phil Oiler's wedding day. I think he and Phil were wandering around down there, and found the noose."

"And what, decided to take turns trying it on?"

"Authentic Civil War relic," Sam said. "They probably couldn't resist."

He and Dean walked along the outside of the church, following its outer wall toward a back alleyway.

"Careful," Sam said, shining his light on the steel tracks running off into the distance.

"Railroad tracks?" Dean mumbled. "Here?"

"Remember that armored train? It ran right through town—and right past here."

"Crazy," Dean shrugged. "Well, let's go to church."

The clapboard exterior was massive, seeming to occupy limitless space in all directions. Around the back, Sam's flashlight picked out a narrow utility stairwell leading down. A plain white door with a square window stood at the bottom.

Navigating the steps, Dean bent over and picked up a loose brick, wrapped his jacket around it, and punched it through the glass. The window burst and glass tinkled down inside the door. Dean reached through—avoiding the shards—found the knob and turned it.

Feet crunching over broken glass, they stepped inside.

Sam went first, shining his flashlight along the walls. Heavy shreds of cobweb hung from the ceiling, and the air was thick with dust. He realized they were standing inside a storage space, a wide, musty room filled with old Bibles and hymnals and racks of choir robes. An old pipe organ towered against the wall, partially disassembled.

There was a sharp clicking noise.

Spinning around, Sam caught a glimpse of a figure leaning over them from above and pointed his flashlight at it.

His heart pounding, he stared at the bloodied face and hands of the wooden statue peering down from its crucifix. The expression on the statue's face was a combination of suffering and infinite gentleness.

"Jesus," Dean breathed. "What's he doing in the basement?"

Sam shrugged.

"Maybe there's been a shift in the dogma."

Dean just gave him a puzzled look.

"Which way from here?"

Sam looked at the far end of the storage room, where several divergent hallways ran out in what looked like a half-dozen different directions. Back at the McClanes' house, Tommy had told them that the church basement was a labyrinth of corridors and sub-chambers, many of which hadn't been thoroughly cleaned out for a century or more.

Half the stuff in the Historical Society came from there, he'd told them. *But there's still whole rooms that people haven't checked out since the Union Army came through. If the noose is anyplace, you'll most likely find it in one of those.*

They kept walking, neither of them speaking. Dean took half a dozen steps forward and stopped, stomping his foot.

"It's metal under here," he announced. "Hollow."

"You mean there's another layer underneath us?"

Dean shone his flashlight down.

"Might be," he said. "It's a heavy metal, too, like iron. Lead, maybe. Except..." He sniffed. "...it smells like ammonia."

"Ammonia sulfate was an early fire retardant," Sam said. "Going back to the nineteenth century. They used it in circus tents and army forts. Somebody had something important to protect down there. See if you can find—"

"A way down?" Dean swung his flashlight directly in front of him, clearly revealing a wide trapezoidal door with a ringbolt. "Like this?"

"Yeah, *just* like that."

They each grabbed the ring and pulled, swinging the trapdoor upward. The steps leading down were ladder-steep and descended so sharply that they had to clamp their flashlights under their arms so they could hang on with both hands to keep from falling.

The steps ended abruptly, and left them standing in a dank and airless cube. The walls were lined with what appeared to be lead, grafted together with bolts and rivets. Tufts of what looked like spider webs festooned the upper edges. From where they stood, they did a slow, circular inspection of the space.

The glow of their flashlights seemed to wither in the outermost pockets of darkness, as if the room itself was sucking the light away in great hungry slurps. Even with the flashlights, there was no way they could see every recessed area at once. Anything could have been waiting for them there.

"What is this?" Dean asked, his voice flat and hollow, as if he were talking inside a tin can.

"It looks like an old operating room." Sam's flashlight found a table with leather restraints and metal buckles. "Aristede Percy's old office, I'm guessing."

"In the sub-cellar of a church?"

"Nobody'd think to look down here, would they? And Doc Percy must have figured that even the Union army would leave it be." His flashlight played along the walls, and he realized that what he'd first thought were cobwebs were actually lines etched into the surface. "Dean, check this out."

"Diagrams." Dean glanced back at Sam. "Doc Percy's amazing rope tricks."

And they were—hundreds of technical drawings, painstakingly detailed, depicting every imaginable type of knot. It was as if Dr. Percy had run through his entire vocabulary of bends, twines, loops and hitches in pursuit of the one true Judas noose.

"I think we're close, Dean," Sam said.

"I think we're more than close."

Dean pointed his light forward, the beam settling in the middle of the room. At the dead center Sam saw a hole in the lead plates where the otherwise seamless surface had been left open to reveal a square of raw black earth, three feet wide and three feet long. The metallic edges of something heavy and square gleamed inside the dirt, a box the size of a tombstone, its exterior illuminated in the same way Beauchamp's coffin had shone—with its own unearthly radiance.

"That's a reliquary," Sam said. "I'll bet that's what the demons were looking for out on the battlefield."

Dean walked over and hunkered down next to it, wiping the dirt away.

"Someone's been down here recently. It's already been dug up, removed, and put back in."

Sam bent down beside Dean, found a long metal handle on his end of the box, and they both pulled. The reliquary came out of the dirt without much resistance, and they set it on the lead floor.

"Be careful," Sam said.

"If this is just full of more bones, I'm gonna be so pissed," Dean said.

Together, they lifted the lid.

It wasn't full of bones.

The brass interior of the box was so intricately engraved with tiny lines of text and symbols that it reminded Dean of circuitry, the prehistoric ancestor of the modern microchip. Looking at the lid made his head throb. It was as if his mind was trying to take in all the thousands of lines of tiny words without his eyes realizing it—as if the codes and charms of the reliquary were actually leaping fully formed into his consciousness.

He shut his eyes and turned away.

Get out, he thought, shaking his head hard. *Get the hell out of my head, box.*

"Dean," Sam's voice was saying. He sounded shaken as well. "Look."

With a grunt, Dean opened his eyes again and looked down, careful to avoid the reliquary's inner lid. In the middle of the box, curled like a snake on red velvet, he saw the noose itself. Thick, rough rope, stiff with age, its knots dark with a century and a half of spilled blood.

"So that's it," he said. "That's the noose that Aristede Percy tied."

"It really does have seven coils," Sam said, lifting the noose up and holding it. "Except the seventh one's hidden, see? It—"

He froze, the flashlight slipping from his hand, striking the lead-lined floor and rolling in a lazy half-circle to the wall.

Dean aimed his own flashlight at his brother. Sam was staring at him wide-eyed, the noose still held loosely in his fingers, his expression a portrait of sheer, unvarnished panic, its message horribly clear: *I can't breathe.*

Under his chin, a ring of shadowy indentation rippled against his throat, squeezing off his windpipe, as if invisible tension wires were cranking tighter into his skin. Sam's eyes bulged, mouth opening and closing, unable to produce more than muted glottal clicks.

He fell to his knees.

"Hang on, Sam. Hang on, bro. I'm gonna cut you out of this thing, once and for all."

Being careful not to touch the noose, Dean used his flashlight to knock it from his brother's hand. It hit the floor with a heavy *thwop*, as if it was sopping wet.

Wedging his flashlight under his arm, Dean reached back to the sheath on his belt, groping for the demon-killing knife.

But the sheath was empty.

The knife was gone.

TWENTY-ONE

On the floor of the room, Sam was helplessly staring up at Dean. His face, formerly white, had begun tingeing a cyanic shade of blue as the first signs of irreversible oxygen deprivation sank deeper into his features.

Finding a loose handle, he picked the noose up and dropped it back into the box. Then Dean whirled around and splashed the white beam of his flashlight around the room.

When did I lose the knife?

Wouldn't he have heard it, if it had fallen out of his pocket onto the metal floor?

What if I lost it earlier? Outside, or up in one of the other rooms?

He looked back at the floor. Sam was tilting slightly to one side now, unable even to sit upright. The look of panic had started sliding away, along with his sense of awareness.

Dean hunched down and lifted his brother back up, searching for a spark of life in his eyes.

He's going to pass out, a mental voice yammered. *He's not getting any air. I have to do something.*

He flashed hard to something an ambulance driver had told him once.

When you're dealing with a choking victim, you don't have time to mess around. Time is brain.

There was no time to go looking for the knife.

Desperate, out of options, Dean swung his brother in front of him, wrapping his arms around him from behind. He made a fist with one hand and locked his other hand around it, thrusting up and into Sam's diaphragm.

At first nothing happened.

Dean did it again, harder.

Sam made an abrupt hiccuping croak and something flew up and out of his mouth, landing on the floor with a clank.

Sam whooped in a deep, rattling breath.

"You all right?" Dean asked tautly.

Sam managed a weak nod. His eyes and nose were streaming with tears, and dirt streaked his face like warpaint. For a moment he looked about six years old, freshly fallen off his bike with a skinned knee.

"What..." he rasped. "What came out of me?"

Dean aimed his flashlight over the lead-lined floor, training it on the small, wet leather pouch that lay five feet away from them. Its drawstring had come open. A few tarnished silver pieces lay scattered around it, gleaming there like flat, incurious eyes.

"Thirty pieces of silver—shekels of Tyre," Dean whispered, turning his attention back to the reliquary. "The noose..."

There was a faint clinking noise. He twitched the flashlight back at the bag of silver pieces again.

"Dean?" Sam's voice came hoarsely. "What...?"

From the far corner came a shuffling noise.

"We're not alone down here," Dean said.

He looked at the spilled coins.

A long, slender hand dipped out of the darkness and plucked one of them up.

Dean jerked the flashlight upward to reveal a bearded face, grinning wildly at them.

The figure stepped forward. He was tall and skeletal, and except for his thick black facial hair, his skin appeared almost unnaturally white and smooth. But moist as well—less like porcelain and more like the flesh of a mushroom. From the emaciated hunch of his shoulders, a colorless, shabby-looking cloak hung down to the floor, its hood thrown back. The hem of the figure's robe dragged on the floor.

"I believe this belongs to me." Kneeling, the figure began to scrape the silver coins up, depositing them carefully back into the satchel from which they'd spilled. The satchel then disappeared under the cloak.

"Judas?" Dean whispered in disbelief.

"No. I'm more of an aide-de-camp." The man looked up again, and this time Dean saw his eyes, their orbits stained an absolute, soulless black.

"Great," Dean said. "Another scum-sucking demon. Just what we—"

"I am *not* a demon." The figure's arms shot forward, taking hold of Dean's throat and jerking him off his feet and straight up into the air. His flashlight slipped from his fingers and went out. There was a weightless, spinning moment in the dark when Dean had time to think, *This is gonna hurt*, and then something flat and hard—the floor, the wall— collided with his skull, ringing it like a bell.

His vision doubled, then tripled. Constellations—whole galaxies of stars—rattled through his head, and when he tried to sit up, all he could taste was the coppery trickle of his own blood.

"You sure... you're not a demon?" he croaked.

"I'm a Collector," the figure said. "Probably the closest term you have for me is spirit. Except that I inhabit a solid form. Case in point..." He drew back one foot with crazy, stuttering speed and swung it forward, smashing Dean hard in the head.

It was a perfectly placed kick, connecting just above the ear, and Dean felt the world closing down around him fast, like a tent whose poles had been yanked away.

Sam grabbed his flashlight and swept it up until he saw the Collector coming toward him. Its robe swung heavily back and forth, jingling as it walked. As it got closer Sam realized that the garment was loaded with pockets, perhaps hundreds of them, each containing leather pouches and satchels of silver pieces. It had to weigh half a ton.

"Where's Judas?"

"He couldn't make it," the figure responded. "Sends his regards."

"Is this what you do?" Sam asked. "Go around for all eternity, picking up blood money?"

"At least I didn't trigger the Apocalypse," the Collector replied. It smiled. "Not that I'm complaining. My employer is back on the A-list again. Suddenly everybody wants the noose—humanity, lesser demons, witches." He shrugged, clinking. "It's a bull market on betrayal."

Sam looked around. There was only one weapon he could see in the room. He picked up the reliquary and threw it as hard as he could at the creature.

Laughing, the Collector ducked.

The box slammed off the wall and landed between them. The Collector stepped over it and blurred toward him, one arm pinioning forward. When the punch connected, it was with the full weight of all the metal loaded in the sleeves, as if the thing's entire body was packed with the silver it had been gathering.

Sam's head jolted backward and bounced off the wall. He dropped the flashlight. Every ounce of light in the room was now gone.

But he could hear something, a sound he recognized.

The scrape of metal against metal. It was a thin, hard sound, and when Sam looked up, he actually saw a few sparks flying along the floor. It wasn't much, but it was enough for him to glimpse, however briefly, the tip of a gleaming steel blade in the Collector's pale hand.

"Did you really think that I would just let you traipse into my house," the voice in the darkness murmured, "with your filthy little weapon?"

A sharp beam of light burst out from the doorway, illuminating the room around them.

"What makes you think it's your house, you son of a bitch?" Tommy McClane's voice asked.

TWENTY-TWO

Through concussion-glazed eyes, Sam gazed back at the steep stairs leading up and out.

Tommy was standing in the doorway with his flashlight pointed at the Collector, while Nate flanked him, his own flashlight steady in his small hand. Neither of them made a move to come any closer.

Smart guys, Sam thought foggily. *You don't want any part of this.*

"Sam?" Tommy said. "Dean? You two okay?"

Dean didn't answer, but Sam sat up and looked at him.

"Okay's not exactly the word I'd use," he said. "You were supposed to go home after you dropped us off."

"It's 'Bring a Friend to Church Day,'" Tommy said, but he didn't take his eyes off the figure standing in front of him. Sam saw the demon-knife clearly now, still shining in the Collector's hand. "Give me the blade," Tommy said, "and the noose."

The Collector made a brief clucking sound that might have been a laugh.

"If you want it so much, come in and get it yourself."

"We don't have to."

"That's what I thought." The Collector shook his head. "You have no idea what you're dealing with."

"I guess we'll see about that," Tommy shrugged. "Go ahead, son."

Still standing in the doorway, Nate reached into his back pocket and pulled out a piece of yellow parchment, unfolding it nimbly and pointing the flashlight at it. It looked very big in his hand.

He began to read.

The incantation was a mix of French and Latin and some other lyrical language Sam didn't recognize. Nate's high, sweet voice make the words sound almost like a song.

"What's this?" the Collector asked.

"Hoodoo binding charm."

"I'm honored," he said. "Unfortunately, as long as I'm able to block it out with the sound of my own voice—"

Sam saw Dean rise up behind the cloaked figure. Dean was holding the noose's reliquary over his head, and he swung it down with a sharp, hard *bang*. The Collector tumbled forward, the blade flying from his hand, his pockets spilling open, his robe ringing out with loads of spilled silver coins.

"Block *that*, you son of a bitch," Dean grunted as Sam grabbed the demon-knife. "Do it, Sam."

Sam didn't need to be prompted. He raised the knife and

shoved it down into the Collector's chest.

The Collector screamed, thrashing, but didn't flash out.

"Moneybags was telling the truth," Dean said. "Not a demon. Oh well. I guess that's—"

The Collector jerked upright again, his face a howling tunnel of rage and violence, and lunged at Sam with both hands.

His fingers locked around Sam's throat, holding him at arms' length as he had with Dean when he'd endeavored to crush Dean's windpipe.

Sam's reaction was pure instinct. His right hand came straight up, driving the demon-knife hard and fast. The thrust planted the blade back in the Collector's chest, in the area where Sam presumed the heart would be, if the Collector had one. The figure shrieked, a strangled, failing cry, and Sam stabbed him again, twice more, until the Collector fell.

Hitting the floor, he lay totally still.

Panting, catching his breath, Sam stepped back, watching for any further sign of life. But there was none forthcoming.

"What about the noose?" Tommy asked from the doorway. "Just don't touch it with your bare hands."

"Yeah, we figured that out." Sam handed the knife to Dean, then bent down, hands still trembling a little, and cut a strip of fabric from the Collector's cloak, wrapping it around his palm like a glove. Duly protected, he lifted the noose from the floor—it seemed somehow heavier than it should have—then fired a glance at Tommy.

"I hope you've got transportation out of here. I don't want to hold onto this thing any longer than I have to."

TWENTY-THREE

It was 3:05 a.m. when Jacqueline Daniels walked into her office, switched on the light, and saw the man standing next to her desk. He had been waiting there in the dark for her, and for a moment she was so surprised that she couldn't speak.

"You," she managed.

The man stood perfectly still, looking back at her with dark-eyed intensity. The trench coat he'd been wearing earlier hung open, and she couldn't see any kind of weapon in his hands or on his person.

Somehow that made him seem even more dangerous.

"How did you get in here?"

"Please sit down."

"Who are you?"

"We need to talk."

Daniels felt a surge of adrenaline in her temples, a sensation like hot coins being pressed on either side of her head. After the collision out on the road, she had spent the rest of the day out looking for the Winchesters. The FBI had joined in the manhunt, and their involvement had only made her job more complicated.

"We need to talk," he repeated.

"You're under arrest," she told him. "That stunt out on the highway today is more than enough reason to lock you up."

Turning, she started away from him, but the man raised one hand and the door slammed shut in front of her face.

"Now please sit down," he instructed.

Daniels turned back to face him. She dropped the pretense of ballsy, hard-case female law enforcement. It was replaced by something somehow harder—an air of cold, almost clinical detachment.

"You have no idea what you're dealing with," she said flatly.

"My name is Castiel."

"I don't care what you call yourself." Walking back to the desk, she reached around for her handcuffs and felt a sharp sting of pain fork up the back of her neck, the result of the car accident earlier. "You think you can just waltz in here, into my office, and start ordering me around?"

"This is bigger than you."

"Nothing in this town is bigger than me." She brought the cuffs forward, but Castiel caught her wrist and held it tightly. With a quick, effortless flick, he turned it over to reveal the tattoo imprinted on her skin. He touched it lightly.

"This sigil won't protect you."

A flicker of doubt wavered over Daniels' face, and then

was gone.

"You like that?" she said. "I got it at Mardi Gras, spring break twelve years ago. Dumb kid stuff, I know, but..."

"You're lying to me."

"What if I am? Why should I care what you think?"

"Time is short," Castiel said. "I need the Witness. Judas. Where is he?"

Daniels shook her head.

"I haven't got the faintest idea what you're talking about."

"You know about the noose. It disappeared twice while it was under your care." His eyes flicked down at the sigil again. "I know that mark."

She said nothing.

"Direct me to my Witness," he demanded. "I won't ask again."

The sheriff didn't move, allowing Castiel to hold onto her hand for another moment, the Santeria tattoo hovering between them like some small but vital lie that had been found out.

Then, unexpectedly, she smiled, and drew her hand back from him.

"Ask all you want, Castiel... or whatever your name is. Poke around my head. Make yourself comfortable. Stay all night." The smile disappeared. "I don't know anything."

Castiel's entire face tightened. Although he didn't actually move forward, he seemed to get both larger and somehow more imposing until his presence filled her entire field of view. His voice trembled with barely suppressed rage.

"I am an Angel of the Lord," he said. "Simply being here has cost me valuable time. Time that I will never get back. *This is important.*"

Daniels stepped back, her eyes widening, feeling her autonomic nervous system respond—sweat prickled under her arms and her pulse quickened in her throat, where she could feel it pumping in her neck. Then she forced herself to calm down again.

"If you really were an angel," she said, like a stern mother facing an errant child, "you wouldn't need me to point you in the right direction, would you?" She shook her head. "Sorry. This is my town. My people have been here since long before you arrived, and we'll be here taking care of things long after you leave." She blew back a wisp of hair that had fallen over her eyes. "Now if you're done with the questions, I'm going home to take some aspirin. Some douche bag wrecked my car today, and I've got one hell of a headache."

Castiel reached out, his fingers brushing her forehead, almost casually.

"It's about to get much worse."

Sheriff Daniels opened her mouth to answer, and then clapped it shut again. Her mind was flooded with images and sensations—blinding light and threatening darkness, righteous anger, walking the battlefields of history, and grace, divine grace.

"I won't ask again," Castiel said. "Where is the noose?"

This time Daniels didn't hesitate. Although she didn't realize it, she had fallen to her knees, and her voice—not ballsy, not anymore, not at all—was spewing out the words without so much as a qualm.

"The church. It's in the basement of the church," she said.

By the time the overwhelming sensations had finally faded, leaving behind the mother of all migraines, Castiel was gone.

Making her way slowly to her feet, Sheriff Jacqueline Daniels staggered the rest of the way to her desk chair and collapsed into it, cradling her face in her hands.

She could scarcely bear to think of what she'd done.

TWENTY-FOUR

Sam and Dean left the church the way they had come in. Father and son followed the Winchesters out of the door without comment. Tommy's pickup was parked behind the rear entrance, Sam climbed into the front seat, sitting in the middle and still holding the noose.

A footstep scraped in the shadows behind them, and Dean turned to see Castiel stepping out of the alleyway.

"Whoa." Tommy raised his flashlight. "Who the hell are you?"

"Easy," Dean said. "He's okay."

"Where is he?" Castiel's eyes were locked on the noose in Sam's hand. His voice was tight with urgency. "Did you see him?"

"The Witness?" Dean shook his head. "Sorry, Cass—he sent his stunt-double. A Collector. Guy didn't know squat."

"We'll see what he tells me," Castiel said, brushing past

them on his way down the stairs, toward the back entrance of the church.

"Ah, Cass...? I don't think that's gonna happen either."

The angel stopped and looked back. "What?"

"Sam kind of... killed him."

"*What*?" Castiel glared at him, appalled. "What were you thinking?"

"It was him or me," Sam said from the cab of the truck.

"I don't think you realize what this is going to cost us," Castiel said. "Neither of you do. Your selfishness might have cost us our last chance."

"His selfishness kept him *alive*," Dean countered.

Castiel's expression of thinly veiled outrage didn't change. He seemed to be on the verge of saying something—perhaps a great many things. In the end he simply turned and descended the back steps.

Tommy exhaled.

"Should I ask?"

"No," Dean said. With a shrug that was more tired than resigned, Tommy crossed the alley to where the pickup was parked and opened the passenger door for Dean.

"It's okay," Dean said, "let the kid ride up front. It's the middle of the night."

"You're in worse shape than he is," Tommy said. "Besides, he's got something back there to keep him occupied."

"You mean, like a game?"

Tommy gave a distracted nod.

"Something like that."

They drove away from the church and down the empty, moonlit alleyway. Tommy steered easily through town, glancing at the noose that Sam still held on his lap, carefully protected by the swath of torn fabric. On the radio, the Marshall Tucker Band was playing 'Can't You See.'

"It's funny," he said thoughtfully, "you hear stories about something for your whole life and when you finally find it, it's almost a let-down, you know?"

"We need to destroy it," Sam said. "Sooner rather than later."

"On the battleground," Tommy said. "That's where it's got to happen."

"Why there?"

"Because that's where it was first tied. Aristede Percy put it together in a medical tent. Used the same knots that he used to stitch up the corpse of Jubal Beauchamp."

Dean's phone chimed. He pulled it out and looked at the screen.

"Huh, must have recovered from its dunking in the swamp," he said, and hit TALK. "Hey, Bobby."

Sam watched his brother peering at the blade in his hands while listening to what Bobby was saying.

"Bobby, what's happening, man?" Bobby's voice was a buzz, the words not clear enough to make out. "What? Yeah, we did." He looked over at the noose on Sam's lap, and then at the blade again. "We're getting ready to do it now. Out on the battleground." He raised an eyebrow at Tommy. "How much further is it?"

"We're almost there," Tommy replied. "See?"

Outside the window, the hillside loomed in the moonlight, though the first hints of pre-dawn light were appearing in the east. Sam could just make out the shapes of tents still spread out across it, between the craters. He remembered what Sarah had said about the re-enactors refusing to leave camp until somebody explained what had happened to their compatriots.

"So yeah, we're..." Dean stopped. "*What?* Say that again?"

The pickup crunched across the parking lot and came to a halt. Before Sam could ask what was happening, he heard something thumping in the back of the truck. The tarp that had covered him and Dean on the way back from the swamp was shifting around. There was a clatter of commotion underneath it, like kicking feet or thudding fists. Sam peered over his shoulder, but it was too dark to see what was happening.

"Tommy? Is Nate okay back there?"

"Oh yeah," Tommy said. "He can take care of himself."

"Are you sure? He's only what? Eleven? "

"Wait a second," Dean cut in, his voice sharp with urgency, "Bobby says we're *not* supposed to cut up the noose. He says if you do that—"

Something in the back of the truck screamed.

TWENTY-FIVE

Dean jumped out and ran around the back.

He grabbed the tarp and ripped it back. What he saw beneath it took several seconds to understand. There were two figures struggling in the shadows, one pinning the other down, smashing its victim with a series of fast, brutal punches. The screams grew louder, more intense.

"Leave him alone!" Dean shouted and gripped the attacker around one arm, swinging him back. As the figure spun around, he realized that the arm he was holding onto belonged to Nate McClane.

"What...?"

The boy gave him a savage grin. Dean turned to stare at the half-conscious face of the victim looking back from the bottom of the truck. He realized that he was looking down at Sarah Rafferty.

"Sarah?"

She groaned, lips barely managing to shape the words. "Help..."

"What did you do to her?" Dean asked, spinning back around to look at Nate.

The boy was still grinning, his lips peeled back to reveal every tooth in his mouth.

His eyes flicked black.

Up in front, both doors of the pickup flew open. Sam jumped down and a moment later Tommy McClane stepped out on his side, sidling unhurriedly toward the back of the truck.

McClane's grin matched his son's. The insides of his eyes seemed to have filled with thick black ink. A shroud of moonlight lay over him like an unearthly cowl.

"We took the girl to play with," McClane said, "just for fun. Kind of a nice reward, don't you think? Sure as hell beats an e-book."

"You did all this just so you could get your hands on the noose?" Dean said.

"Let's just say that Judas and his Collectors were a little too selfish when it came to letting everybody have a turn with it," the McClane-demon sneered. "So me and my kin just started looking around for it ourselves."

Dean thought of the demons they'd encountered on the hillside, and the ones out on the country highway.

"Your kin."

"We've got plans," McClane said. "Big plans."

Dean shook his head.

"Dammit! I *knew* I had you pegged right the first time."

"We could never have set foot inside that room." McClane nodded. "But you did it for us." He glanced at the Nate-demon. "Go ahead. Finish her off."

Nate lunged toward Sarah Rafferty with a snarl. Sam grabbed him by the shoulders and slammed his face into the side of the truck. The demon's head bounced off and slumped away.

He felt something ripped away from him and realized that the noose was gone—he'd lost it when he'd grabbed the demon.

McClane had it now. Almost faster than Sam's eyes could process, the demon lashed out with it, looping the coil around Dean's wrist and yanking the blade from his hand.

Sam started to charge toward McClane, and pain exploded through his head from behind, blasting his vision into a kaleidoscope of shattered rhinestone. When he staggered around, he saw Nate grinning at him again, rubbing his fist. And behind the demon, he glimpsed Sarah crawling away, inching slowly, painfully, away into the darkness.

Off to his left, McClane had Dean on his knees and was kicking him. Dean struggled to his feet and McClane kicked him again, harder. The cold clatter of his laugh was like someone spilling a bag of marbles across a museum floor. There was nothing human in it.

"You ready?" he asked, and Nate nodded. The look of unwholesome eagerness scrawled over the boy's face was almost obscene.

Raising the knife, McClane stuck its tip into the first of the noose's coils, shoving it upward. Sam heard a ripping noise as the blade tore through the weave of the hemp.

Black ooze spurted from the rope like drainage from an infected loop of bowel, trickling down McClane's hands and up to his elbows.

Seeing it, Sam remembered how heavy the rope had felt, and realized that was because it was alive and pulsating, nearly sloshing in Tommy's hands. He stared as the black substance rose up, shimmering in the night air, moving the way they'd seen it move in the back of the morgue van.

The Moa'ah.

It swirled over their heads and flung itself outward, across the battlefield and up the hill, a streak of greater blackness against the gloom that preceded sunrise.

A sudden eruption of thunder shook the world, lights flashing and shivering over the hillside, illuminating the full curvature of the landscape in a series of silent-movie flickers.

No, Sam realized, *not thunder.*

Guns.

Up on top of the hill, figures began to appear, manning the siege howitzers that the state police had not been able to bring down. More of them rose up every second.

They seemed to be rising up out of the ground itself.

But they weren't—the meat-suits they wore were the bodies of the re-enactors who had refused to abandon the battlefield.

* * *

"Ah." Reaching the final loop, McClane changed the angle of the blade, as if anticipating greater resistance. "The seventh coil. Now you're going to see why Judas wants to keep the noose so closely protected."

Dean swung at him.

It should have worked. McClane wasn't even looking at him—he was still apparently absorbed by the task at hand. But when Dean's fist came at him, McClane switched hands with the noose, then reached up almost casually and gripped Dean by the wrist, swinging him around sideways and applying pressure to his radial nerve.

A thin lancet of icy-hot pain sprang up Dean's arm and his knees went out from under him, dropping him to the ground.

"Nate?" McClane called out. From inside the cab of the truck, Nate stepped out holding what Sam Winchester recognized as a Civil War musket from the gun rack. Wielding the gun with ease, the boy aimed and pulled the trigger. There was a flat, eardrum-rending report as the muzzle-flash ignited the air in front of him. Dean flailed backward, twisted and was landed face-first in the dirt.

"Dean!" Sam shouted.

McClane turned and eyed him speculatively.

"I hope you're gonna be a little tougher to crack," he said, drawing the demon-blade, tipping it back and throwing it at Sam at point-blank range.

TWENTY-SIX

Jacqueline Daniels' head continued to throb mercilessly.

It was four in the morning and she was still in her office. She had called her deputy, Jerry, in from the stakeout at the Winchesters' motel. He had arrived along with Sergeant Earl Ray Harris and a handful of State Troopers, plus an FBI agent.

She couldn't tell them about the noose, or the thirty silver pieces that she'd removed from the battlefield, or her recent excavations in the basement of the First Pentecostal Church of Mission's Ridge.

She definitely couldn't reveal the recent visit from the self-proclaimed angel in a trench coat who had called himself Castiel. And besides, even if she told them the truth, none of them would believe her.

"Let's go over what happened out on the highway again," said the FBI officer, a slicked-back thirty-something careerist named Andrew Tremont. In the last hour or so, Sheriff Daniels had silently upgraded Agent Tremont's status from localized pain-in-the-ass to world-class hemorrhoid as his questions had become less random and more focused on how and when her particular investigation had fallen apart.

Also, he was drinking her coffee—the good stuff, the French Roast that she normally kept hidden under the microwave.

"You said someone stepped out in the middle of the road, in front of your cruiser, and forced you to stop. You have reason to believe this person was working with the two men?"

"I already told you that—we're just wasting time," Daniels said. "Besides, I'm not the one under investigation here."

Tremont lifted his mug to his lips and sipped noisily.

"May I remind you, Sheriff, that you called us."

"To help me catch a couple of men who were impersonating Federal Agents, not to pick my investigation to pieces."

"I submit that our goals might not be mutually exclusive." Another two ounces of premium coffee disappeared into Tremont's mouth. "Now, two of our DMORT workers claim they saw you taking something from the corpse of Phil Oiler and placing it in a bag," Tremont said. "One of them said that it jingled."

"Jingled?"

"Like coins. Can you tell me anything about that?"

"That's right. I stole a bag of quarters from a corpse." Daniels knuckled her eyes and waited for one of the State

Troopers—or even her own deputy, for that matter—to stick up for her. Jerry hadn't even had the consideration to stay awake.

When none of them spoke, she glared back up at the Fed.

"Look, Agent Tremont…"

"That's a very interesting tattoo on your wrist, Sheriff. Might I ask after its provenance?"

"Its what—?"

BOOM!

Everybody jumped up and scraped back their chairs.

"Not again," Jerry moaned, sitting up in the seat where he'd been drowsing.

Tremont stiffened, then stood, wiped the spilled coffee from his shirt cuff and put the cup aside, heading toward the front window to look out onto the street.

"Who do you have stationed out at the battlefield?" Daniels asked Sergeant Harris.

"Two details," Harris said. "At midnight they were still trying to get those re-enactors to leave."

Nobody else spoke.

They headed out.

TWENTY-SEVEN

Sam ducked the blade.

It hissed past his head like a low-flying comet, and when he came up again, both Tommy and Nate McClane were barreling toward him. Nate had discarded the gun and was circling about looking for the demon-killing knife.

BOOM!

The skyline erupted with the biggest explosion yet, heaving up vast ripples of convulsed air that blew back Sam's hair and made the pickup jounce sideways on its shocks. He sprang up into the back of the truck, kicked out the window above the gun rack, and yanked down the shotgun and the canister of salt.

He broke the weapon open, dumped in salt and worked the action.

He pointed it down at Nate.

The boy froze.

"Please, mister." All at once the young face went smooth and innocent, becoming that of an average kid—one who'd stumbled in far over his head. His eyes had changed from black to a pale blue, and they were filling with frightened tears. "You don't know what it's like."

Sam took a breath.

"Yes," he said, "I do."

"Just give me a chance."

It's a trap. And if you fall for it, you're an even bigger idiot than I thought.

Still…

Sam hesitated. The shotgun felt very heavy in his grip now. He lowered the gun a fraction…

And the Nate-demon lunged for him.

Sam had the shotgun back up instantly.

He pulled the trigger.

The barrel roared, a storm of rock salt blasting from its muzzle, tearing the demon down. A child-sized raft of living smoke came shrieking out of Nate's skin, and somewhere off to the left, Sam heard Tommy McClane start to scream. Obscenities spilled from his lips, curses in a dozen different languages. Sam didn't wait around to hear the translation.

Squirming through the broken back window into the pickup's cab, he dropped into the driver's seat. The keys were still in the ignition. He cranked them, dropped the truck into reverse, spun the wheel and floored the gas, flinging the pickup back around.

Up ahead in the headlights, he saw Tommy McClane

staring straight at him.

But Dean was gone.

Pinned by the headlights of the oncoming truck, the thing that called itself Tommy McClane stood his ground.

He'd lost the last coil of the noose somewhere.

This wasn't the plan, gunning the Winchesters down in the middle of the battle before the endgame was achieved. But the plan hadn't included the sight of his son being shredded by a shotgun full of rock salt either. When the demon had seen that...

Oh, when he had seen that...

McClane's jaw tightened. Rage lay heavy against his heart like the flat surface of a branding iron. He wasn't thinking straight. He cast around quickly for something to throw and came up with a short timber post that had been dislodged from somewhere. He hurled it with all his strength at the truck. The glass crazed on impact, and Sam Winchester ducked reflexively, but then quickly sat back up behind the wheel.

McClane could see Sam's face through the windshield, and it was a mirror of his own anger.

At the last second, he dove out of the way, letting the pickup squeal past him.

Sam swerved across the parking lot and spun the pickup around. He couldn't see Dean anywhere, and he was running out of time.

Up on the hill, the siege howitzers were blasting to pieces

whatever remained of the night. The onslaught was so unrelenting that it was impossible to discern the gunfire from the echoes. In the east, the glow of dawn shuddered along the rim of the Earth, low and red and trickling through the treetops, as if the sky itself was bleeding from the attack.

Sam steered the pickup around again, heading for the battlefield, the tents and the trees. Somewhere off to his left he could make out the Civil War steam locomotive by the old railway shed. Between the explosions, over the pickup truck's engine, he heard screaming.

He looked over at the figures in uniform, storming down the hill. Some wore blue, others gray. They were running down the incline side-by-side regardless of sides, like the fulfillment of some ancient prophecy.

And behold, the Yankee shall campaign with the Rebel.

All carried authentic-looking Civil War weapons. And although Sam Winchester couldn't know for sure at this distance, in this misty, smoke shrouded pre-dawn light, he had the sick feeling that every single one of them had the same onyx-black eyes.

He thought of what McClane had said.

"My kin."

Dean, he thought miserably, *where are you?*

Up ahead of him, men had already come out of the tents. Re-enactors—the ones whose bodies the demons hadn't possessed—were standing in their skivvies and long underwear and gaping up at the wave of figures storming down the hillside. The pickup's headlights strafed their faces, revealing the slack disbelief of sleepers who'd awakened from a nightmare only to find that the nightmare had followed them into reality.

There was another artillery flash from above, the boom following instantly afterward, the long shadows of the attackers flickering forward over the grass and down like the fingers of some unthinkably vast and clutching claw.

"Look out!" Sam palmed the pickup's horn and held it down. Its nasal beep was absurdly small against the roar of battle. "Get out of here! Run!"

The pickup hit a bump and slammed violently upward, coming down hard on its shocks with a suspension-busting crack. Sam saw the tents and the men, the trees and creek and the hillside beyond it, all of it closer now, but his brother wasn't there, wasn't anywhere, and if he didn't find him soon—

A figure burst out of the trees in front of him, darting through his headlights, fifteen feet away. Sam had just enough time to recognize her, the name kiting briefly across his conscious mind—

Sarah Rafferty.

—when the biggest howitzer shell yet hit the pickup head-on, blasting it sideways and up into the air, pinwheeling Sam Winchester with it, out of the blue and into the black.

The truck hit the ground, torn open and bleeding flame.

It was exactly five a.m.

TWENTY-EIGHT

Get up.

It was his father's voice. Dean would have recognized it anywhere. Even if the old man hadn't been standing directly in front of him, gazing down, looking supremely unimpressed with the string of events that had led up to this.

I can't, Dad. A jumble of impressions and responses floundered ineffectively in Dean's mind. *I'm shot. Son of a bitch shot me. You saw it.*

What I saw was a man get blindsided by his own stupidity, John Winchester responded unsympathetically. *I saw a man who—given his circumstances and the sheer latitude of his folly—is lucky he's not dead.*

Dad, how come you're talking like Abraham Lincoln? Dean thought, and that was when he realized that his father was actually *dressed* like Lincoln, right down to the beard and stovetop hat. Despite the searing, white-hot pain in his chest and right shoulder, the idea struck him as absurdly funny. Here he was, balled up in the edge of the parking lot, trying to staunch the flow of blood from the grapeshot that had come flying out of a vintage Civil War musket. With no less than the Great Emancipator himself, as real as he'd appeared in Phil Wagner's wax museum, towering over him.

Dad...?

Dean reached up.

Fought to stand upright.

And touched cold metal.

Lincoln, his father, was a statue.

Not a man at all. A bronze likeness. Craggy and hard. It stood on a concrete base overlooking the battlefield, one hand extended permanently northward, as if pointing out to Mission's Ridge the cause of its inevitable loss.

Dean felt the world pivoting away from him on greasy hinges, and all equilibrium fled.

Then he was actually clinging to the statue, gripping Honest Abe's arm to hold himself upright.

How much blood have I lost anyway?

Sirens howled in the distance, approaching at speed. Above them, Dean heard the screaming—the Rebel Yell coming down the hillside, although all it reminded him of was whiskey and Billy Idol.

His brain struggled to take it all in.

Tommy McClane had grabbed the knife and he'd unleashed... this.

Dean narrowed his eyes and saw the pickup truck—

Tommy McClane's truck, the traitorous bastard—swerving madly across the grass of the battlefield, between explosions. Whoever was behind the wheel looked like they were driving with their feet.

But where's Sam?

The question blazed a new line of clarity across his thoughts, temporarily anyway, long enough to realize that what he was dealing with was essentially a flesh wound, and wasn't that a nice deceptive turn of phrase? *Only a flesh wound.*

And just like that, here came Harvey Keitel in *Reservoir Dogs*: *Aside from the knee cap, the gut's the worst place you can get shot. It hurts like hell, but you ain't dying.* And good God, would the pop culture stuff *ever* stop coming, even in moments of profound physical agony?

Now red and blue bubble lights were flashing across the parking lot. Sheriff's vehicles.

Cops.

"Great," Dean muttered. "Perfect. It's gotta—"

THOOM!

Off to his right, maybe less than a hundred yards away, an artillery shell hit the Ford's backbed, blasting it sky-high, spinning it up into the air like a Matchbox car whose youthful owner had lost interest in it.

In the startled hush that followed, he heard tires screeching, spraying gravel. Doors opening. Voices. Cop voices.

"It's you," a voice said.

Dean let go of the statue's arm and staggered around to find himself face-to-face with McClane. The bastard was no longer armed, but in all honesty, Dean didn't suppose he would even need a weapon now. McClane could poke him with a sharp stick and get the job done.

Bull. I ain't dying.

"We just killed your brother, by the way," McClane was saying. "He was in that pickup when it went blooey." A grin, utterly inhuman, spread over his face. "Payback for what he did to *my* partner."

"Sent him back to Hell?" Dean said. "Good. But you're lying about Sam being dead."

"What makes you say that?"

"You worked too hard for this. And Sam's too important to you."

The demon paused, as if for reflection, and did an odd thing—he nodded.

"You're right," McClane said. "He is."

"So what's this all about? With you and your 'kin?'"

McClane waved the question away as if it didn't concern him.

"Wheels within wheels. It's all too sophisticated for the likes of you."

"You know," Dean said, "I think I liked you better when you were just a redneck."

"Ah," the demon beamed—but was there a flicker of impatience behind that placidity, a flame of anger buried deep in the demon's enamel of bemused calm? Dean thought so. Seeing it there gave him a dose of vicious satisfaction.

"In any case, we're past all that now aren't we?" McClane tilted his whiskered chin toward the shredded skin of Dean's right chest wall. "How's the shoulder, by the way?"

"Hurts like hell."

"Good."

Dean ignored him. He was looking beyond the demon now, at the police cars with their strobes flickering over the parking lot, where no less than Sheriff Jackie Daniels herself was striding toward the battlefield, radio in hand, leading a phalanx of State Troopers. There was another crashing *BOOM* as the sky exploded again, and they all stopped in their tracks.

Fixing his eyes back on McClane, Dean stood up straight.

"So what's the plan?"

McClane cocked an eyebrow.

"I beg your pardon?"

"You kill me and my brother, then your demon army takes over the town and throws a big party. Fly the Confederate flag, play war heroes. Am I missing anything?"

"No," McClane said. "I think you've unfolded it all very nicely."

"What happens when Judas catches up with you?"

"It'll be too late."

"Yeah," Dean said. "You're right about that."

McClane cocked his head.

"You agree with me?"

"Absolutely."

"Why?"

Dean shook his head.

"Because me and Honest Abe here are gonna kick your Rebel ass."

Something snapped in the demon's composure. He charged Dean in a single blurring step, flying at him, knocking him flat again. Dean tasted the familiar now sulfuric tang of asphalt.

Hello, asphalt.

McClane stepped over him and swung back his foot, kicking him in the shoulder.

Right in the gunshot wound.

The pain was unholy. Nerve bundles shrieked inside him. Dean screamed. He couldn't help it. McClane kicked him again.

The demon was talking between kicks. Spitting out words in bursts, between swings of his boot.

"When I tortured Winston to death—"

Kick.

"I thought it couldn't get any more fun than that."

Kick.

"But *this*—"

Kick.

"Makes *that*—"

Kick.

"Feel like a dryhump in the backseat of old granddad's Studebaker."

Dean squirmed at McClane's feet. The tips of the demon's Red Wing boots were dripping with his blood. A glob of it dangled from one of the half-tied laces. He tried to scream again but couldn't. His entire right side had gone numb, and that included his face. Being numb, however, somehow didn't stop it from feeling as if it were on fire.

McClane towered over him, triumphant. Dean could see him drawing back his leg, preparing one last kick, the blow that would either knock him unconscious or snap his spinal cord.

"Goodbye, Dean."

The boot arced forward again. This time, somehow, Dean managed to reach up with his good arm and seize hold of it, clutching onto it for dear life. The move was so sudden, so unexpected, that it actually caught McClane off-balance, and when Dean jerked him forward, the demon went sprawling with a half-audible grunt of surprise.

Straddling him, Dean grabbed McClane by the hair and rammed his face down into the pavement. Something splintered; something popped. Facial bones. Cartilage. Teeth.

Remember, an inner voice cut in, *this is just a meat-suit, there once was a person in there—*

At the moment Dean didn't care. He struck the McClane-demon again, hard and fast, while he still had the momentum. Capsules of adrenaline were erupting in his motor cortex, bursting open like strings of firecrackers, popping hot wires of energy through the muscles of his good arm.

Beneath him, McClane let out a muffled howl and spat a mouthful of pebbles and debris, and it was like music to Dean's ears. All at once he felt as if he could do this all night if he had to.

"You worthless piece of trash," McClane said. "Look

what you did to my face."

The demon pitched over to one side, throwing Dean down, and locked both hands around his throat. Dean looked up at McClane. His face was a cratered, oozing ruin. McClane's grip pinched off Dean's trachea, and he couldn't breathe.

Blackness started sliding down on top of him in a massive avalanche.

Then, screaming.

But this time it wasn't him.

McClane was screaming.

The hands around Dean's throat loosened and fell slack. The bloody oval of the demon's mouth was wide open and he was howling bloody murder. Behind him, Sheriff Jackie Daniels was standing over his shoulder, reaching down, doing something to the back of his neck. From this angle, Dean couldn't quite see what it was... and when he did see, it didn't make sense.

The sheriff was holding the inside of her wrist against McClane's neck. Not hitting him, not even grabbing him, barely even touching him. But it was enough to make McClane collapse, cringing, onto his belly, where he cowered and whimpered and tried to pull away but couldn't. Daniels hunkered down next to him, pressing her wrist directly against his flesh.

She wasn't looking at Dean. Didn't even seem to notice he was there. Every ounce of her attention was focused on Tommy McClane.

"Struggle all you want," she said. "As long as this tattoo's on you, you're not leaving this meat-suit. So tell me what I want to know." She leaned further down, until her face was right next to his head. And although her voice wasn't loud, Dean could hear, very clearly, the words she spoke in McClane's ear.

"Where's the noose?"

TWENTY-NINE

When Sam came to, he was being dragged backward by his arms across the burning battleground. One of his boots had come off and his ankle was swollen to the size of a grapefruit. Migraine-sized throbs of pain rocked his vision, sloshing his thoughts from side to side.

Groaning silently, Sam looked behind him. The two men pulling him were also re-enactors, one Union, one Confederate. The Rebel was shouting into a cell phone. The Yankee had a first aid kit.

All around him, the world blazed. Men in Civil War uniforms were running wildly, erratically, in every direction. More uniformed figures—McClane's demonic kin—were screaming down the hillside, weapons held up and ready. It was impossible to say how many of them were out there, although he thought there might be a hundred, maybe more. They seemed to be spilling out of a wound in time, boiling out of some dusty epoch whose daily life was as remote as the pages of history itself. Yet they were real enough.

As Sam watched, one of the demons ran up to a re-enactor in a blue Union uniform and plunged his bayonet into the man's throat, then yanked it out with a howl of triumph and thrust the blade, still dripping, high into the air. The first rays of morning sunlight kissed the gleaming tip and shot back a sunburst of scarlet brilliance.

Sam's head reeled.

Then he remembered the pickup truck.

And Sarah Rafferty.

The truck he could see from here, fifty yards away, a burning heap of twisted metal that had crashed at the edge of the creek. Flames from the cab had spread to engulf the stand of cypress trees, and although it was probably just the reflection of the flames, it looked like the creek itself had caught fire.

But what about Sarah?

And Dean?

Sam had fallen out of the driver's seat when the mortar round had launched it into the air. Thinking back, he recalled how much it had hurt when he'd hit the dirt, with just enough consciousness left to look up and see Tommy McClane's Ranger spinning in the air over his head, its twisted front-end grinning down from the peak of its arc, just before gravity snagged it and flung it back down.

He had glanced over, seen Sarah's face as she'd stuck her head up and realized what was falling toward her —

After that: blackout.

Yanking Sam's arms, the two re-enactors dragged him into a tent and dropped him unceremoniously next to several other men who were already sprawled on the ground, motionless, bleeding through their uniforms.

"Can you hear me, buddy?"

Sam raised his head.

"Yeah."

"You all right? Anything broken?"

"I don't think so." He looked around. The tent smelled like scorched wool and had the coppery stink of freshly spilled blood. There was the sickeningly sweet smell of cauterized flesh, too. The man lying to his immediate right had had all his hair burned away, leaving his scalp a boiled globe of fresh scars and blisters. One of his ears was almost burned off. He was weeping and throwing up at the same time, trying to breathe and calling out to someone named Megan.

"This thing doesn't work for crap," the Rebel re-enactor said, finally tossing the cell phone down in disgust. "Can you see the parking lot?"

"They've got it blocked off."

"Sheriff's out there somewhere," the Yank said. "I saw her car. Plus the Staties."

"What about ambulances?"

"They—"

A blast of musketfire tore through the tent wall, opening a hole the size of a dinner plate in the fabric. Through it, Sam saw the grinning faces of demons in blue and gray approaching from fifty yards away. From what he could see, they had formed a barricade around the encampment, blocking off the parking lot and encircling the remaining tents on all sides.

"They're closing in," the Rebel said. "Who *are* these guys?"

The Yankee didn't look back.

"Their eyes are all black," he said. "And the weapons they're using are replicas. How is that even possible?"

"Long story." For an instant Sam considered trying to clarify, then decided against it. "We've got to get out of here."

"There's no other place. Those things have the parking lot blocked off. We're surrounded."

"Doesn't matter—we can't stay here." Levering himself up, Sam counted the other men in the tent and came up with eleven. "Who else is out there on the battlefield?"

The Confederate shrugged, a jerky, panicky move, like a hostage under interrogation, and when his Adam's apple jerked up and down, Sam realized that he'd met the man before.

"You're..." He hesitated, grasping for the name. "Ashcroft, right?"

"Ashgrove."

"You're part of the 32nd. I talked to you before." Sam cast his eyes back out through the hole in the tent. "Is there anybody else left alive out there?"

"Not many," Ashgrove admitted. "Most of them took off

for town before they sealed off the camp, or..." His voice broke off, and he looked abruptly as if he were going to burst into tears. "My God. What's *happening*?"

"We have to get these wounded men to safety," Sam said. "Now." He found a boot that would replace the one he had lost, and pulled it on. He had a feeling its owner wasn't around any longer to miss it.

Ashgrove shook his head.

"We're staying here."

"In a *tent*?"

"It's shelter. Maybe if we leave 'em alone, those things will pass us by."

Sam flicked his eyes back. He saw a pile of canvas stretchers, the old-fashioned kind with wooden poles on either side.

"If we stack the wounded by twos, we can get them out of here while there's still a chance. Otherwise..." He swallowed, tasting something sour in his throat and belly, "we're all going to die."

The Union boy looked Sam straight in the eye. He looked tired and frightened but, like Ashgrove, determined to deal with the practicalities of survival.

"Say we can get out," he said, "Ash is right. We're surrounded. Where are we going to go?"

Sam opened his mouth and realized he didn't have an answer.

"I know a place."

The three of them looked over at the entrance of the tent.

Standing there, clutching the canvas flap in one hand, was Sarah Rafferty. Her face was strained, and the bruises under her eyes made her look like the victim of a particularly inept undertaker, but it was definitely Sarah, upright and breathing. Sam felt a small gust of relief, a sense that something might actually go right this early-morning.

"Sarah," he said, "are you...?"

"I'm alive."

"Sarah?" Ashgrove asked, staring at her. "Wait, Tanner—? You're a girl?"

Sarah waved him off.

"There's a place we can get to," she said.

THIRTY

Judas Iscariot strolled along the hillside.

He'd considered making his entrance on a pale horse, but that seemed too pretentious, even for him. Simply appearing here tempted fate in a way that wasn't entirely comfortable with. Time and experience had made him circumspect.

But in the end he'd donned a general's uniform, strapped on a cutlass and strode out from the copse of live oak along the battlefield's southernmost perimeter to watch the action unfold from above. Not because he intended to alter the flow of events—such things were better left to others—but simply to observe the endlessly amusing spectacle of human suffering.

Like crucifixions and pornography, it never got old.

He'd arrived before dawn, already hearing the sound of cannons and the cries of demonic jubilation down below. It didn't do much to lighten his mood. News of what had happened to his Collector in the basement of the Pentecostal Church had, of course, already reached him and left him feeling sour, plunging him into the restlessness and depression that had plagued him on and off for the last two thousand years.

He'd always been the moodiest of the Twelve, and becoming a demon hadn't changed that.

And then there was the loss of a noose.

There were other nooses, of course, a half-dozen of them, scattered throughout the world from Bangkok to Burbank, most in the hands of private collectors or occultists with no real sense of what they had. And there would be more, as humanity in its endless resourcefulness decoded the secret of the seventh knot and wove their fates like the obedient little sheep they were.

But now there was one less.

And losing a noose and a Collector in one night—to a minor demon like McClane—was an aggravation to Iscariot. At least the battle that the idiot had unleashed here would—

"Judas?"

He stopped, brought up short by the unexpected sound of his name spoken aloud. He turned to look at the man standing a few yards away, wearing a rumpled suit and trench coat, looking as if he too had been up half the night. Recognizing him at last, Judas smiled.

"Castiel," he said, with genuine pleasure. "How are you, my friend?"

Castiel stared at him.

"I've been looking everywhere for you."

Judas turned his attention again to the battle below.

"Always a treat to watch the ants swarm the anthill, isn't it?" When Castiel didn't respond, Judas turned and scowled a little. "Surely you don't hold me accountable for this."

"It was your noose."

"Stolen from me!" Judas protested, more petulant than angry. "McClane and his minions ambushed one of my Collectors and took it from him. Worse, he had your friends do it for him."

"Yet it was your noose, so it becomes your responsibility."

Judas shook his head, holding up both hands.

"I didn't survive as long as I have by getting involved in every petty skirmish that comes along."

"This isn't just another petty skirmish," Castiel said. "With everything that's been happening, you must know what's at stake."

"Again, it's not my problem."

"You're not worried?"

Judas frowned at him.

"Of course I am. You know me. I *always* worry." He paused to watch a squadron of demons on horseback set fire to a tent. Several human re-enactors came scurrying out and the demons shot them in the back with muskets. He could hear their laughter, brittle and barbed. "But honestly, when you look at the grand tapestry, what's to be done?" Then he turned again.

"Why are *you* here?" Realization, of a sort, began to sink

into Judas's face. "What is it you want from me, Castiel?"

"It's not like that."

"Don't try to be tactful. It was never your gift."

Castiel sighed.

"I'm looking for Him."

"Still?"

"Still."

"I don't see why—" Judas broke off. "Wait. You don't think... that *I*...?" He gaped at Castiel, eyes agog, mouth slightly open. The sense of incredulity swelled into full-blown disbelief, straining all color from his cheeks. For a moment he felt as if he was going to explode with anger.

Instead he burst out laughing.

"Oh. Oh my." The laughter doubled him over, and he held his stomach, roaring until tears sparkled in his eyes. "Oh, my dear Castiel, I'm sorry, I... I saw you here and I just assumed that you were... but you... Oh my—"

And he was off again on a flight of giggles.

"You should see the look on your face. Priceless." When he finally caught his breath, he clapped Castiel on the shoulder. "Thank you," wiping his eyes, sniffling, "I needed that. I honestly did."

Castiel stood stiffly, unmoved.

"Did you not break bread with His son?"

"Oh, yes," Judas said, gazing skyward, apparently lost in reverie. "Yes indeed. We broke bread and I knelt at his feet. And we talked of many things." His head snapped around, voice sharp, eyes hard and black. There wasn't a trace of laughter remaining in his face. *"But I serve a different master now."*

Castiel took a step back, cringing away.

"Sorry. Painful memory." Judas stepped forward and reached out to brush an imaginary bit of lint from Castiel's shoulder. "Go. Go down. Be among your people."

Your people.

Castiel turned to look reluctantly back down the hill at the ruined battlefield, thick with smoke. What he saw there was Hieronymus Bosch by way of Ken Burns. Demons on horseback and on foot had surrounded the last of the re-enactors' tents and were spreading across the parking lot. They had fallen on the police cars and were smashing their windows, rocking the vehicles back and forth, setting fire to them.

A dozen additional state police cruisers arrived, and troopers began firing back at the attackers from behind their vehicles. One of the demons jumped his horse over a police car, swinging his saber down in a wild Pete Townshend-style swoop to lop the arm off the trooper below him. The horse's hooves smashed the cruiser's roof-lights, throwing showers of sparks across the pavement. Below him, the maimed trooper stood gaping at the jetting stump where his arm had once been.

"I came to speak to you," Castiel said.

Judas affected a tone of sympathy.

"Then I'm sorry for your wasted trip."

"It's not wasted if I can help," Castiel said, "and I will. But first I have to know if you've told me everything you can. You must tell me what you know."

"I know this is difficult to hear," Judas said, "but knowing what I do know about Him, I can honestly say that you should be grateful for your ignorance. It truly is bliss."

Castiel looked at him. It was impossible to tell whether the demon was joking or not. Whatever the case, Judas was right. And he needed to get down there, and now, while there was still something left to save.

"Castiel?" Judas called out behind him as he resumed his patrol. "It was good to catch up. Don't be a stranger."

THIRTY-ONE

Dean wasn't exactly sure when they started losing the battle, or if they'd ever been winning. But when he saw the first wave of demons in uniforms spilling over the parking lot, picking off cops and re-enactors with lethal accuracy, he realized that the outcome was no longer even in doubt.

In front of him, still on the pavement, McClane was laughing.

"You like that?" Sheriff Daniels asked the demon, staring straight down into its ruined face. "You want some more, you soulless prick?"

McClane couldn't speak, but just lay cackling with a big hysterical-looking grin twisting up the corners of his bloody, ruined mouth. Most of his teeth were gone, and those that remained stuck up every which way like tombstones in tornado country. His bright, black eyes were flashing everywhere at once... everywhere, that was, except for at

Sheriff Daniels, who leaned over him again, holding up the inside of her wrist, this time toward his face.

Dean looked at the Santeria tattoo on the Sheriff's wrist, the loop of numbers with the smaller circle within it. It wasn't exactly glowing, but there was a peculiar *luminescence* to it, as if the lines themselves were heating up from inside. It reminded him of the glowing dial on one of those old-time radium wristwatches, the kind that was rumored to give you cancer.

"Hey, Sheriff, what——?" Dean started.

"Quiet," the sheriff snapped, never taking her attention away from McClane. "I'm going to ask you one more time. *Where's the noose?*"

McClane grinned harder, the remains of his teeth gnashing together. Tendons bulged in his jaw.

"I cut it up. Chopped it to pieces. Cast it to the four winds."

"You're lying." Bending down, she peeled back McClane's left eyelid so that the black sclera was completely exposed. "Hold him," she said to Dean. "Pin him down."

"What?" Dean said. "So now we're BFFs?"

"If your definition of a friend is someone who's saving your ass," Daniels said, "then yes. I still don't understand who the hell you are, but right now I'm your only hope."

"And dozens of other golden hits," Dean retorted. "Sorry, Sheriff. I'll take my chances."

"You don't have to trust me. Just do as I say. I'll explain later. All right?"

"Do as you *say*? *That's* your pitch?" Dean stared at her in disbelief. "Screw you, lady."

He crawled away, moving slowly, but definitely moving.

The ground was littered with broken glass, fallen branches and debris. He bumped into something and, before he knew what was happening, felt a hand taking him by the arm, lifting him gently but firmly back to his feet. He wobbled a little, but felt steadier when he saw who had helped him up.

"Cass," Dean said. "Nice of you to get in the game."

Castiel nodded.

"I found this for you," he said, and Dean saw that he was holding the demon-killing knife.

Dean took the blade. Its familiar shape and heft felt good in his hand. He looked back to where the sheriff was still struggling to hold McClane down and felt the angel's hand on his shoulder.

"She's right, Dean."

"What?"

"Sheriff Daniels. She and her family bear a sacred trust—they have been guardians of the noose for generations."

"Look, Cass, I know you're probably still a little creased about Sam capping your Witness and all, but..."

"That doesn't matter now." Castiel's grip on Dean's shoulder tightened considerably, almost painfully. "My priorities have changed."

Then the angel disappeared abruptly.

Sighing, Dean tucked the blade into his belt and started back toward McClane and the sheriff. She glanced up at him in surprise.

"Changed your mind?"

"I don't wanna talk about it." Squatting down, he used his good arm to hold McClane's upper torso and shoulders flat against the asphalt. In front of him, close enough that he could smell her shampoo, Sheriff Daniels leaned directly over McClane's wide-open eye. Then she flexed her hand back and pressed the tattoo directly against his eyeball. Dean heard a faint hissing sound, like a red-hot brand burning into skin, and McClane shrieked and thrashed.

"*Where is it?*" Daniels asked, shouting above his screams. "Where's the seventh coil?"

She held her wrist there for another moment, then drew it away. Underneath her, McClane gasped and fumed. When he looked up at them, Dean saw the faint imprint of her tattoo burned over the glassy black eightball of his left eye. It looked like a tiny, complicated blueprint. Reddish-black tears trickled from the corners.

"...lost it..." he managed. "...dropped it somewhere..." He manufactured another grin and somehow managed a weak, watery laugh. "Doesn't matter... you've already lost... stupid bitch..." He sucked in his cheeks, and made a *horking* noise deep in his throat.

"Look out," Dean said, "I think he's gonna—"

The demon spat a thick gobbet of blood directly in the sheriff's face. She didn't even flinch, just reached up and wiped the spittle from her cheek. Throughout it all, her expression didn't change. When she spoke again her voice was as cold as ice.

"That's it," she said. "I'm going to burn your eyes right out of your head."

From nearby came a loud nickering scream, a clatter of hooves on metal, and Dean looked up to see two black-eyed Confederate demons on horseback riding hard across the roofs of parked police cars. One was carrying a flaming Confederate flag. Upon seeing Dean and the sheriff, the soldier drew back his arm and threw it, the pole whistling through the air like a javelin in the direction of Sheriff Daniels.

Dean sprang upward and grabbed Daniels, knocking her backward just as the pole slammed into the asphalt where she'd been less than a second earlier.

Daniels gazed up at him, startled and badly shaken. The demon's blood was still streaked along the side of her nose.

"Idiot."

"You're welcome," Dean said.

The sheriff pointed at the bloodstain where McClane had been lying.

"He's gone."

"You still owe me a big explanation."

Daniels seethed.

"So do you. Get *off* me!"

Another clatter of hooves filled the air, and they both looked around to see the next wave of demons surging across the parking lot.

"There's no time," Dean said, hauling himself to his feet. He glanced at the cruiser nearest them. Its roof was partially smashed in, the lights and windshield demolished, but the loudspeakers on either side still looked operational.

He started toward the car, opened the door and got in the driver's seat.

"Wait," Daniels said. "What are you doing?"

"I've got an idea."

"You can't leave."

"I'm not going anywhere," Dean said. "But my left arm is shot. You're gonna have to help me steer."

THIRTY-TWO

Six-fifteen a.m.

While the rest of the Eastern seaboard was just waking up, pouring its first cup of coffee, switching on the news and getting the first online updates of what would soon be called the strangest attack in recent history, other events were beginning to unfold.

Less than two hours had passed since Tommy McClane had cut the noose open, unleashing his armies of the night upon the town of Mission's Ridge. But in this age of modern marvels, with the country's threat level parked semi-permanently on orange, two hours was plenty of time.

Word had gone out.

Alarms had sounded. Officials had been shaken from their beds and briefed. And certain federal agencies had responded with the appropriate degree of vigor and enthusiasm.

Since 9/11, the federal Department of Homeland Security

had authorized the existence of several regional top-secret domestic taskforces—standing armies with state-of-the-art weapons and ground and air support. Unlike the National Guard, these soldiers trained for the single eventuality of a full-blown terrorist attack on U.S. soil. When the map turned red over Mission's Ridge, Georgia, that morning at six a.m., they were on the ground and mobilized immediately.

Sam and Sarah were running across the battlefield as fast as they could, with a stretcher pole in each hand, when the first black helicopter buzzed overhead. Sam paid it no attention. At the moment he was far too busy to care.

The height discrepancy between him and Sarah made carrying the stretcher difficult enough; the weight made it nearly impossible. Balanced on the stretcher were two of the wounded re-enactors from the tent, one of whom didn't look as though he'd survive the trip. Ashgrove and the other re-enactor, a young man named Bendis, were running behind them, carrying two more on their stretcher.

The rest, they were going to have to come back for—if they even got that chance.

"This way!" Sarah shouted. "Watch out for the rails!" Crab-walking, she and Sam scrambled over the railroad tracks, stepping over heavy wooden cross-ties, behind the steam engine, the coal car and flatcar of the old nineteenth-century train. Beyond it, the railway shed stood along the western edge of the thick second-growth forest that marked the outer perimeter of the battlefield.

The helicopter circled back over the woods, completing a circuit of the perimeter.

Backing up to the railway shed, Sam swung his foot and kicked the heavy wooden door wide open, then he and Sarah ducked inside. The shadows smelled like coal and oil and ancient iron.

"The roof's re-enforced steel," Sarah said. "The C.S.A. did it to protect their trains. I thought we might be safer in here."

"Good." Sam nodded, wincing as they put the stretcher down.

"Are you all right?" she asked.

"My ankle… I'll be okay."

Ashgrove and Bendis were already coming through the doorway with their wounded, laying the stretcher down as gently as possible.

"What about the others?" Bendis asked.

"I can try to go back," Sam said, and overhead he heard the low-flying helicopter making another pass, the roar of its rotors temporarily blotting out everything else.

"Did you guys see that thing?" Bendis asked. "Who was that?"

"Whoever it is," Sarah said, "they're not here to help us."

"Maybe it's FEMA," Ashgrove said.

Bendis shot him a look.

"Bite your tongue."

"Come on, man." Ashgrove shook his head. "It could be medevac. If we can get up on the roof—"

A thunderous explosion shook the railway shed, rattling

the walls like the inside of a steel drum, dropping a thin rain of dust and debris from the rafters. Sam dropped into a defensive crouch. When the aftershock passed, he made his way back over to the doorway and looked across the battlefield, still crouching low.

His heart sank.

"It's too late."

Sarah joined him and gazed across the battlefield. The tent that they'd left behind just minutes before was in flames. The last four re-enactors had never made it out, and now they never would. The demons that had set fire to it were riding horses around the blaze, firing into it at random.

Overhead, the chopper roared by again.

Standing up, Sam took a brief inventory of their new surroundings. The railroad shed was perhaps two hundred feet by thirty. Like the town's Historical Society, it had been refurbished with small exhibits illustrating the battle that had taken place. Display cases containing railway tools, newspapers, and other relics adorned the walls.

On the floor in front of him, Bendis and Ashgrove hunched over the wounded, performing triage to gauge the severity of their casualties.

"Man," Bendis said, "this is worse than Fallujah."

Sarah glanced at him.

"You were there?"

"Two tours. That's where I met this douchebag." He glanced over at Ashgrove. "Eighteen months and not a scratch. Then last year he calls me up and asks if I want to have some fun over the weekend." Bendis shook his head sourly. "Some fun."

Ashgrove gave him a cold look.

"You saying you want to quit, Marine?"

Bendis stood up. His cheeks were flushed.

"Negative. Whatever's out there, whatever the hell it is, is trying to take us out. Two of those guys that died out there are men that you and I served with."

"Good," Ashgrove said. "I was starting to worry about you for a second."

Either these guys are really brave, Sam thought to himself, *or really stupid*. Then he joined them in tending to the wounded.

Another explosion rocked the earth. The railway shed shivered around them. More rust-colored debris sifted down.

Sam bent down over one of the wounded men. The re-enactor's leg had been almost completely severed just below the knee, and was hanging by the barest shreds of integument, and Sam's hands were gloved in blood. He lifted the red-soaked rags from the leg, tossing them aside in a sloppy, dripping pile.

"Hey!" he suddenly shouted.

"What is it?" Sarah asked.

"Tourniquet." Sam glanced at Ashgrove and Bendis. "Which one of you guys tied this on?"

"I did," Bendis said. "What's it matter?"

"Where did you find it?"

"Out there somewhere. It was a piece of rope and I grabbed it. His femoral artery was severed and I needed something to hold the bandage on, stop the bleeding. What's the difference?"

Using strips of gauze to hold it, Sam studied the thick loop of rope pulled tight around the man's leg.

It was the last coil of the noose.

Sarah leaned closer to look.

"What is that?"

The man sat up and grabbed her. His eyes were open and pitch black.

He grinned.

Sarah screamed.

THIRTY-THREE

Staggering across the battlefield, McClane heard a scream.

He was weak, blind in one eye, his meat-suit wracked with pain, but none of that mattered. The chaos he'd unleashed here was reaching its boiling point, and soon the goal would be in sight. The cannons that had been blaring from the hillside had finally fallen silent, perhaps temporarily, maybe for good. It didn't matter. The objective was now within reach.

Sam Winchester's true purpose would be fulfilled.

Grinning through cracked lips, McClane heard another scream—this one louder.

It came from the railway shed.

He glanced at the parking lot, saw both flanks of his demonic army riding back around to surround the police cars and military vehicles that now filled the lot.

Soldiers in camouflage were piling out of the newly-arrived personnel carriers, carrying automatic rifles, opening fire on the

Confederate and Union-garbed figures. The demons charged them, cutting through their ranks, blasting and slashing with high good humor. Their antique muskets, breechloaders and carbines had become supernaturally powerful, spraying flame that enveloped whole vehicles in great, leaping gulps.

A soldier jumped out of a blazing Humvee and bolted across the parking lot. The man was on fire and screaming. As the recon helicopter blared back overhead, a cavalry demon went charging up behind the burning man and decapitated him with a swift slash of his bayonet. In one fluid movement the demon caught the severed head in midair, its face and hair burning like a Roman candle, spun around in the saddle and flung it upward at the helicopter.

The burning missile smashed into the chopper's glass canopy, shattering it, and a moment later, the cockpit was filled with orange flame and smoke, the helicopter pitching and yawing erratically in the air. McClane paused to watch as the chopper canted hard to the left and fell out of the sky, exploding on the ground in a fireball that unleashed heat he could feel from where he stood. Good times.

He raised one hand in the air.

It was as if a silent alarm had sounded across the battlefield. The cavalry and infantry demons stopped what they were doing, swinging around to face him.

Hundreds of attentive black-eyed faces looked directly at him, shoulders at attention, awaiting orders.

McClane pointed at the shed.

THIRTY-FOUR

Sam landed on the demon full-force, with the idea that sheer momentum might be enough. Obligingly, it let go of Sarah's neck. Only to turn its attention to Sam. Instantly it was on him, and it was out for blood.

He had no plan and no means of self-defense.

The demon pinned Sam to the floor. The sulfurous stink was overwhelming. It grabbed one of the bloody rags that had served as its tourniquet, jerked Sam's mouth open and tried to cram the rag inside.

Sam choked, his gag-reflex triggering over and over, and managed to get his mouth shut. Even so, he could smell the blood. But not just any blood. It was heavy, almost intoxicatingly potent and somehow rotten at the same time—demon blood. The re-enactor had continued seeping into his bandages long after the noose had turned him.

He tried to turn his head, to keep his mouth shut, but the

demon had fastened its hand over his lower jaw and kept trying to pry it open.

In the background, a million miles away, something was happening. Ashgrove and Bendis were scuffling to get the attacker off of him. The demon shrugged them away, batting them off like insects.

Sam couldn't see much. The room was fading fast around him, sinking away in gradations of gray.

"*Leave him alone,*" a voice said.

The demon jerked upright, his weight rising off Sam's chest. As his vision cleared, he saw Castiel had yanked his assailant away from him and was holding the demon by the throat, both hands clenching while the demon made gargling sounds.

"Cass," Sam choked. "I thought—"

The door of the railroad shed blew off its hinges, flying inward, smashing the demon backward and flinging it across the room like some unwanted toy.

Castiel vanished.

In the middle of it all, Sam felt a random verse from Scripture race through his mind: *And the stone the builder rejected will become the cornerstone.* Where did these thoughts come from, he wondered dazedly, and why did they arrive in his mind when they did?

The door was followed by the rest of the wall, the wood and reinforced steel of the shed itself blasting inward on a geyser of flame as wide as a semi. That gout of fire sucked the oxygen out of the building. The ceiling pulled downward in a crumpling shriek of splintering oak and tortured steel. It was like being trapped inside an enormous tin can as it was being crushed.

The roof's coming down, Sam thought, *And it—*

The noise stopped. The last row of crossbeams held steady.

Sam stared up at the steel plating, partially caved in five meters above their heads.

Forcing himself up, he spat the bloody rag from his mouth. He jabbed one finger down his throat, felt his stomach tighten and squeeze, and expelled a thick spew of bloody liquid, spitting it out onto the ground.

Did I get it out?

I think so. I hope so. I guess we'll find out soon enough.

Through the smoke, he saw Tommy McClane walking through the fire. McClane's face was a mad Expressionist painting of bruises and insults. One black eye flickered with an imprinted sigil that seemed to have been burned directly onto his optic membrane. He was flanked by more demons than Sam could count, all of them armed with sabers, muskets, and bayonets, and when the back wall of the railway shed began to crumple and collapse, Sam saw that they had encircled it on all sides.

"We've been waiting a long time for this," McClane said. "I think you're ready now."

"What do you...?"

"Your true nature. I'm aware that it requires a certain amount of carnage and a heightened degree of desperation to bring it forth." McClane's one working eye rolled upward, weirdly detached from the other. He nodded over at the demon that had shoved its bandages into Sam's mouth. "He was trying to do it himself, but he didn't really know what he was doing. And besides, I had to see it with my own... well, eyes."

"What?" Sam asked. "What are you talking about?"

"You. You're his vessel. Say *yes*. Bring him forth."

"Lucifer?"

McClane nodded.

"That's what this is all about?"

"You *will* be the Light-bringer, Sam." Suddenly McClane was standing directly in front of him, bare inches away. Within breathing distance. It had happened so fast, in a parody of motion, that Sam didn't even see him move.

"Certainly you're aware of the Gnostic gospel. *If you bring forth what is inside you, what you bring forth will save you. If you don't bring forth what's inside of you, what you don't bring forth will destroy you.*" He smiled, almost gently now. "So I present you with the choice. Manifest your true self for me now, or be destroyed."

"You make it sound so tempting."

"Tempting or not," McClane said, "it's the best offer you're going to get, and it's not going to get that good again."

Sam shook his head.

"Then I guess you'd better kill me."

McClane just looked at him, a faint smile still riding the corners of his lips. He didn't even appear to be upset. If anything, he seemed satisfied.

"First things first." Gesturing at one of the cavalry demons to his left, he said, "Kill the girl."

"Wait," Sam started. "She's not—"

The demon's arm snapped forward, grabbing Sarah Rafferty by the hair and jerking her toward him, the edge of his bayonet resting against her throat. Sam could see the throb of her pulse just beneath her skin, reflected in the mirror-brightness of the blade.

"Care to try again?" McClane asked. "No?" Then, to the bayonet-wielding demon. "Go ahead. Take your time."

The blade bit in to Sarah's neck. Sam saw her mouth leap open in a startled dark oval of pain.

But the noise he heard this time wasn't a scream.

It was his brother's voice.

THIRTY-FIVE

"Deus, et Peter Domini nostri Jesu Christi, invoco nomen sanctum..."

The state police cruiser hit a bump, and through the shooting pain Dean gripped the microphone harder, holding it to his lips. He could hear his own voice broadcast through the loudspeaker on top of the cruiser. The volume was turned up as loud as it could go, crackling out where the whole world could hear it.

"et clementiam tuam supplex exposco: ut adversus hunc..."

"Is it working?" Daniels shouted.

Without pausing to answer, Dean pointed out at the partially collapsed railroad shed that lay straight in front of them, sixty yards away. The sheriff gunned the accelerator, tearing up clumps of scorched battlefield dirt, swerving to the right and then bringing them back on course.

The demons surrounding the railroad shed were already

recoiling, falling off their horses, collapsing to the ground in waves. They threw back their heads, wafts of thick vapor spewing out of mouths, wrenching their bodies into convulsions as they departed, swirling upward. The atmosphere around the shed was beginning to stain with a thick and sooty patina of airborne grime, like the polluted sky of a Midwestern factory town.

"Keep going," Daniels said. "Don't stop."

Dean didn't stop.

"et omnem immundum spiritum, qui vexat hoc plasma tuum..."

The *Rituale Romanum* spilled from his lips automatically, without requiring conscious thought. Seeing the bastards go down like this always got him jazzed, triggering each line of Latin so that there was no hesitation, no interruption.

The cruiser swung up in front of the shed, stopping just short of running over the bodies that now lay strewn over the grass in the entryway.

"Over there!" Sheriff Daniels said. *"Look!"*

Dean snapped his head to the side and saw what she was talking about. Some of the demons—whole detachments of them, it looked like—were covering their ears, running and escaping into the woods. So he kept going.

"mihi auxilium praestare digneris. Per eumdem Dominum"

The *Rituale* overtook some of them before they could get out of hearing distance, but others vanished into the trees.

In the meantime, something else was happening.

Some of the Civil War re-enactors—those that *hadn't*

been possessed and were still trying to fight their way off the battlefield—were coming face-to-face with their demon-possessed brothers-in-arms. The result was eerily similar the confusion and chaos that typified actual battles. Dean saw one of them run up to a demon dressed as a Confederate soldier, approaching the man with both hands outstretched in a "you remember me" gesture. The demon's response was to stab the man directly in the heart, dropping him and stepping over his bloody corpse.

Daniels slammed on the brakes, skidding to a halt. Dean finished the first portion of the exorcism. He could see inside the shed now. The demons were gone, reduced to a scrum of foul-smelling murk that was eddying lazily out of the holes in the roof.

Dean jumped out of the car, wincing but not stopping. Through the thick clouds of the demon-smog, he saw Sam slouched over on the floor in what looked like a lake of blood. There was a girl slumped next to him—Sarah Rafferty, he realized. They seemed to be holding each other up. All around them, re-enactors lay bleeding in the dirt, pale and motionless like heaps of gore-stained operating room laundry. It was impossible to say which—if any—were still alive.

Or, for that matter, which ones had died fighting off the demons, and which were evacuated meat-suits that the demons had left behind.

"Sammy!" Dean made his way over. "Oh, dude..."

"It's okay," Sam said. "Not as bad as it looks."

"That good, 'cause it looks pretty freakin' bad."

Sam shook his head.

"What about you? McClane shot you."

"Misfire. Flesh wound."

"Lucky break." He stiffened a little, looked around. "Where is McClane anyway?"

"I must have smoked his ass with the *Rituale*," Dean said. "Figured you heard that part."

"No." Sam's expression was bleak. "McClane got out of earshot before the exorcism took hold. With a bunch of his soldiers."

Dean's eyes widened. "*What?*"

They both looked over at Sheriff Daniels. The expression on her face was a combination of disappointment and alarm.

"They're out there, and they—" she began, then her voice broke off. "*You found it?*" She said, peering past Sam.

She reached past him to the floor of the shed, grabbed a loose stretch of bandage and picked up the last uncut coil of noose from the ground. She held it at arm's length, as if afraid to get too close to it, yet unable to put it down.

"The last loop. It's still intact."

Sam nodded.

"One of the men found it out there. Put it on a wounded soldier as a tourniquet."

"Not a good choice."

"Tell me about it," Sam grunted.

"But..." Daniels was turning the noose over in her fingers, examining it for flaws., "it's good for us."

"What? Why?"

"The seventh coil is the most powerful one in the noose. If we can get it back to its reliquary intact, lock it down in the basement of the church, we can stop the effects of the noose."

"How do you know all this?" Sam asked.

"She's the chosen descendant of the original guardian of the noose," Dean parroted. "Sworn to keep it locked up in a demon-proof room." And, off Sam's perplexed reaction: "I talked to Cass."

"Tommy McClane and I share a common ancestor," Daniels said, "that much, you probably figured out. But power corrupts, and absolute power corrupts absolutely. As much as I want to keep the noose locked away, McClane wanted to get it out—even before he was possessed. He coveted its magic, and it made him an appealing vessel for the lesser demons that took him over.

"I've returned it to the reliquary before, after finding it on Dave Wolverton's corpse." She fell silent a moment. "But what's their endgame?"

"They want me to be Lucifer's vessel," Sam said bluntly. He let the words lie there.

"I beg your pardon?"

"It's a long story," Dean interjected, "and a pretty ugly one."

He drew in a breath, bolstered by what Daniels had told them. "So all we have to do is put the last coil back in the reliquary? How easy is that?"

"Not easy at all." The sheriff gazed out of the open side of the wrecked railway shed, across the smoking battlefield and eastward toward town. "There's still an army of demons between us and the church, ready to do whatever it takes to stop us."

"What about *our* army?" Sarah Rafferty asked. "Those soldiers out there. Can't they help?"

"You've seen what those things can do," Dean said. "What do you think?"

Real hopelessness flashed through her expression, making her look even more pale and exhausted.

"Then what...?" she began.

Sam bent down and picked up a musket.

"We bring the fight to them."

"With what," Dean asked, "replica guns?"

"Demon weapons kill demons, too," Sam said. "I saw it happen, out on the battlefield, when I turned that siege cannon around on one of them." He looked his brother squarely in the face. "And they run on blood. Demon blood."

Dean gaped at him, unable to articulate or even identify the bolt of harsh, vivid emotion that he experienced just hearing those words from his brother.

Anger?

Distrust?

Neither of those words came close. Glancing at his brother, he saw that Sam was experiencing an even more gut-level reaction. He looked paralyzed with fear.

"That's what Rufus told us at the beginning of all this— that the weapons ran on blood," Dean said finally. "He didn't say it was demon blood, though. I hate that stuff."

"You've never tasted it," Sam said evenly.

"So we find a demon," Daniels cut in, "and we make it bleed. Where's the problem in that?"

"You know how it is—there's never one around when you need it," Dean muttered.

Then Sam looked over at the pile of bloody bandages that had been held in place by the last coil of the noose—the remains of the re-enactor's field dressing.

"I think I've got us covered," he said.

THIRTY-SIX

The vision was coming back into McClane's left eye.

It was different, however.

He now saw two different worlds from two different sides of his head. His right eye was normal—as "normal" as a demon's view of the world could be, a subterranean crawlspace of predatory opportunities and constant craven impulses—but his left one had changed dramatically.

Closing his right eye and opening his left, he was greeted by an entirely new landscape, cut out in shades of reddish-orange like scalding bronze from the sculptor's forge. He saw emotions personified in pulsing shades of blue and gray and black.

Riding into town on the back of a horse, pursued by Jeeps and military trucks, the demon that called itself Tommy McClane discovered that he liked looking at things this way—especially human beings. He had escaped the *Rituale*, and he'd begun to relax and regroup.

However, at the moment he was under attack from both sides. Soldiers in half-tracks and Humvees were firing on him and the remains of his demonic retinue, their bullets powerless, and McClane amused himself by squinting through his left eye, watching the auras of the humans, the actual fear in their hearts made manifest in all its glory. He wondered idly what it might taste like.

Opening both eyes now, he watched the world unfold in both directions at once. Spectral figures of his own demonic army, U.S. military personnel, and civilians all swirled together in a miasma of motion and intention. It was a peculiar kind of magic, more illusion than actual power, but a pleasant diversion, and he wished he had the luxury of enjoying it more fully.

But he a town to occupy, and to sack.

He knew, of course, that Daniels and the Winchesters would try to return the noose to the reliquary.

All he had to do was stop them.

It was almost eight a.m. when McClane's hundred-strong demon army rode down the eight-block stretch of storefronts and buildings that constituted Main Street of Mission's Ridge. They rode past the Dixie Buggy Wash and the Twin Kiss and the Ben Franklin Five and Dime. Some of them, like McClane, came on horseback, others on motorcycles or in stolen police cars or military vehicles still stuffed full of dead soldiers. Demons in Confederate and Union uniforms steered while others rode shotgun, firing out of the windows at the last townspeople scurrying for cover on either side of the street.

It was a turkey-shoot, pure and simple, and the demons treated it as such.

"Hey, Captain!" a soldier yelled from McClane's left flank. "Watch this!" Drawing his saber, he flicked his wrist, sending the blade across the street where it hit a man standing in front of a Blockbuster Video, impaling him against a poster for a forthcoming Sandra Bullock romantic comedy. The man twitched and squirmed like an insect on a collector's pin, and then fell still. Closing his right eye, McClane watched the man's aura curdling from bright red to a listless, uninteresting charcoal gray.

McClane giggled, then snorted, then found himself braying with laughter. Setback or no setback, exorcism or no exorcism, there was absolutely no part of this that he wasn't loving with every fiber of his being. He was a demon, and he lived for this. It was Superbowl 666, and he was the starting quarterback.

Straightening in the saddle, he slowed his horse. The First Pentecostal Church of Mission's Ridge lay straight ahead, three blocks down. Seeing it brought new gravity to the moment. It was time for strategy.

"You men take the right side of the street." Then McClane swung his arm toward the other flank. "You all take the opposite side. Get up in those windows. Pick your positions carefully. Minimal exposure, clear line of sight—"

"What's the plan, Captain?"

"I'm turning this place into Dealey Plaza," McClane said. "When those boys come through with the noose, we're gonna go Lee Harvey Oswald on their asses."

THIRTY-SEVEN

Sarah Rafferty grabbed hold of the flatcar and pulled herself up until she was standing next to the Gatling gun mounted there on a turret. Sheriff Daniels was already positioned behind it, inspecting the gun's hand-crank. She grabbed the lever in both hands and struggled to turn it, pushing down with all her weight, but the mechanism was frozen in place.

"You think this is going to work?" Sarah said.

"Do I think..." Leaning out of the locomotive's cab, Dean glanced down at Sam. "Tell 'em, Sammy."

"Tell me what?"

"Dean loves Clint Eastwood movies," Sam said.

Sarah stared at the Winchester brothers.

"What am I missing?"

"Ever see *The Gauntlet*?" Dean asked.

"No, I don't think so."

Dean rolled his eyes. "No appreciation for the classics.

Okay, Eastwood plays a washed-up cop bringing back an ex-hooker who's testifying against this corrupt big-city police commissioner. All he has to do is get the witness back alive. Except the commish has every cop on the force out waiting for Eastwood and they're armed to the teeth, turning the streets of downtown Phoenix into the world's biggest shooting gallery. So Clint shows up on the outskirts of town in a clanking old Greyhound bus that he's tricked out with sheet metal over the windshield, and he and his witness have to run the gauntlet."

He looked at the women expectantly. Sarah and Sheriff Daniels were both staring at him blankly.

Sarah spoke first.

"And this is supposed to make me feel better how?"

Dean started to answer with something witty and sarcastic, when he turned to take his first good look around the steam engine's cab.

Suddenly he wasn't so sure either.

The massive iron boiler in front of him looked as big as a house. Gauges, levers, valves and pipes sprouted out from it in every direction. A chunky thing that looked like an aluminum teapot with a brass handle stuck out by his legs. Down below, the ancient firebox hung open, cold and dead like the mouth of a giant, exhaling the long-lost coal vapors from fuel that had burned up a century before.

Come on. Get ahold of yourself, he said silently. *It's just internal combustion, right? How different can it be from the Impala?*

He grabbed the big lever that ran horizontally across the cab from left to right. It had to be the throttle. Gripping in both hands, he jerked on it as hard as he could.

It didn't budge.

"Uh, Sam?"

Sam climbed through the empty coal car into the cab with the bloody wads of bundled up bandages in his arms.

"You better hang on."

"What? Why—"

Without bothering to answer, Sam shoved half the demon-blood stained rags through the fire door into the empty box, slammed the metal grate, and stepped back.

Nothing happened.

He and Dean stood momentarily silent, looking at it.

"I think when Doug Henning did this trick," Dean said, "it worked out better."

"Hang on." Sam bent down and peered through the slots in the grate. He could see the rags piled up in there. They didn't appear to have changed.

Pulling the fire door open again, he picked up a long iron poker that was leaning against the boiler and stuck it inside, extending it slowly toward the pile of fabric. He nudged it gently, like a kid poking a sleeping snake with a stick.

"I don't get it." He pushed harder, the tip of the poker scraping across the metal floor, throwing up sparks. "Maybe it needs more bl—"

The rags exploded.

It was like a rocket going off inside a tinderbox. Flame

shot out of the fire door in a thick jet of blue headed right toward Sam's face. At the last instant he jolted sideways, the poker flying from his hand, clattering across the floor, and for a dizzying second his equilibrium was gone and he almost fell out of the cab.

Dean's hand swung down and grabbed his collar, pulling him back.

"Shut the door!" Sam shouted. "Get it closed!"

Dean grabbed the poker and rammed it forward, aiming at the grate again and clapping it shut. Blue flames spewed and flickered eagerly out of the slots, writhing like serpents' tongues.

All around them, the railway cab gave a massive shudder and a sharp clank. Dean could hear the sound of old iron as the air around him filled with churning smoke, steam creaking through the engine's pipes, its valves straining under long forgotten pressure. The needles sprang to life on the gauges in front of him, twitching and arrowing upward in great optimistic leaps.

He could see tiny puffs of vapor hissing from the boiler's seams.

Dean clung onto a pipe, felt it growing hotter in his hand until he couldn't hold on any longer. He leaned out of the doorway. One of the women—Dean thought it was the sheriff—was shouting up at him from the flatcar.

"What's going on? Is it working?"

Before he could answer, the locomotive jerked forward.

In July 1938, the locomotive *Mallard* set the land speed record for steam on a run from London's King's Cross station, England, on the East Coast Main Line. Officials clocked her at a hundred and twenty-six miles per hour before the engine's bearings started to overheat and the engineer had to slow it down. "Any more speed, lads," he'd supposedly told his fireman, "and we'd be sitting down for a kip with the Almighty Himself."

When the Winchesters saw the outskirts of Mission's Ridge coming up in front of them, they weren't traveling quite that fast—probably only eighty, although it felt like a hundred up in the cab, where Dean had the throttle all the way open. The whistle screamed steadily overhead. The other valve-control was a hand-release lever called the Johnson bar. A half-mile from downtown, Dean had his Johnson running full-tilt, as well.

Within minutes, they'd be there.

The train rocketed hard down the tracks, pistons pounding, chuffing smoke. It was impossible not to think of it as a living thing. Dean held the regulator steady at maximum as the last of the woods blurred past them, giving way to houses and farms.

"Dean!"

Standing up in the cab, his eyes tearing up from the wind and velocity, Sam had to shout to be heard.

"We have to stop!"

"What?"

"*Stop!*"

"That's crazy! It—"

Then Dean saw why.

Up ahead in the distance, where the first storefronts and shops marked the beginning of Mission's Ridge proper, the tracks were covered with bodies.

And some of them appeared to be still alive.

McClane had gotten the idea at the last moment, looking at the poor bastard impaled in front of Blockbuster. He'd heard the locomotive's whistle shrieking off in the distance and understood immediately how the Winchesters were bringing the noose back to the church.

Kneeling down in the middle of Main Street, resting his hands on the rails, he could already feel them humming.

"Quick!" he said. "Somebody get me some kids!"

They were tied to the tracks.

Dean could see the faces from a hundred yards away, though for a moment his mind refused to accept it. A little blonde girl in a blue dress and white tights, her face a pale porcelain sculpture of pure terror.

Behind her, arms and legs tied, were maybe a dozen other children from town, all looking up and screaming—some silently, others not. His heart froze. A single thought pulsed through his mind—*Where are their parents?*—but the answer was already there, pounding like the wheels underneath them.

Possessed. Or worse.

Dead. Dead. Dead.

Dean grabbed the air brake and yanked it back as hard as he could. Tortured metal howled. The engine lurched hard, its couplings slamming together between the cars, pistons fuming, wheels grinding, dumping off showers of sparks in every direction, but still ramming forward, ensnared in its own momentum.

"There's not enough time!" Sam shouted.

The train scraped on, brake shoes hissing as the locomotive slithered inexorably down Main Street on insufficient friction. They *were* slowing down—twenty, now fifteen miles per hour—but the process was taking too long. Dean stood at the brake, his mouth pinched into an expression of absolute concentration, as if he could somehow stop their progress through sheer force of will.

Sam jumped.

Dean didn't even realize Sam had done it until he saw his brother, not just running, but flat-out *sprinting*, ahead. He saw something flash in Sam's hand, it looked like a pair of pliers, and then he was actually moving along the rails in front of the locomotive.

Reaching the blonde girl tied to the tracks, Sam pushed the pliers down and started snapping ropes, chopping through them as fast as he could. Once freed, the girl sprang up tearfully, and he turned to the next child, a five-year-old boy in a ripped t-shirt and grubby red shorts.

He got the boy's arms free, but his legs were slick with sweat and grease from the tracks, and he wouldn't hold still.

Then Sam got it, and the boy scrabbled away.

He moved on to the next one, but behind him now, he could feel the bulk of the train roaring closer, not just shaking the rails but pounding them, shocking them to life with a steady, awful vibration of unthinkable force and power.

He looked up at the rest of the children. So many of them—too many of them—ten more at least, each tied tightly and separately into place.

They were all staring straight at him.

The shadow of the train swept down. And Sam Winchester understood he wouldn't be able to save them all.

He turned around and looked.

The train was still coming.

Fifty feet away.

Thirty.

Twenty.

He stood paralyzed, riveted to the spot. Fate seemed to be pointing its skeletal finger directly at him. For one illogical moment he considered throwing himself down on the tracks in the hope of providing the last necessary bit of obstruction. Maybe it would save the last kid in line. Maybe it would—

He shut his eyes.

With a final scraping squeal, the engine halted.

He looked up again. It was less than three feet in front of him. He could have reached out and touched the cowcatcher.

"Sam!" Dean shouted, from up in the cab. "Cut those kids loose! We're sitting—"

Then, from the upper windows of Main Street, the first

gunshots rang out.

The adrenaline was on him now, and Sam worked fast, his trembling hands moving with almost superhuman speed. But he wasn't fast enough. Two of the kids were injured, one cut by his pliers, the other hit in the leg by a stray bullet.

When he glanced around, Dean was next to him with Ruby's knife, and they hunched together slashing the ropes in quick deliberate swipes, getting the kids loose and pushing them hard toward the nearest open doors on the far side of the street.

They could feel bits of sidewalk and asphalt spitting up at them as the muskets fired.

Sam didn't need to look up to know what was happening.

Demons were shooting down from both sides, spanking the concrete with a hail of grapeshot.

They're shooting around me, he thought. *They still don't want to harm the vessel.*

When he flicked his gaze up again, he saw the last of the children ducking into the shelter of a restaurant called Whotta Lotta Pizza. Ten seconds later, the pizza parlour window burst apart under heavy gunfire. He hoped—prayed—that the kids were smart enough to stay down.

Hemmed in by bullets and utterly exposed, Sam looked at Dean. He could see the soldiers now and realized that the first fusillade of shots had been playful, meant to instill fear. But playtime was over. They were crouching in windows and standing on top of buildings, and the comparison to *The Gauntlet* wasn't just some rallying cry anymore. It was happening, and they were in the middle of it.

We're dead meat, he thought. *Or at least Dean is.*

Suddenly, from the flatcar at the back of the train, he heard a new sound, a mechanical clanking noise. A steady stream of blasts accompanied it, as if someone back there had just opened up with a machine gun.

What the—

Before Sam understood what was happening, the demons started falling. From above, along the rooftops, they dropped their weapons and were pitching backward in every direction, flung aside in twitching ballistic dances. Sagging, they went limp and then fell forward, plummeting to earth as if they themselves were no more than Hell's own re-enactors, playing out their own Light-bringer's famous descent from grace.

He glanced back at the flatcar.

Sheriff Daniels was standing behind the Civil War Gatling gun, turning the crank with a fierce concentration. The smoking barrels rotated steadily, spitting out a firestorm upward and around. The iron shafts were gleaming with a pale scarlet color where they'd been wiped down with the bloody rags.

Daniels worked the crank faster. Behind her, Sarah Rafferty held the turret of the gun, rotating the sheriff around to spray the upper rooftops.

The sheriff saw Sam watching her, and took one hand off the gun, pawing violently at the air.

"Get moving," she shouted. "Run!"

THIRTY-EIGHT

Lunging back up into the cab, Dean didn't wait for further orders.

He disengaged the airbrake, only peripherally aware of Sam jumping in behind him as he grabbed the throttle with both hands and swung it wide. The train lurched forward on the rails. Bullets rattled and caroomed off the iron locomotive car in a steady clatter of lead.

Straight ahead and four blocks away, he saw the church. Its white steeple rose up into the blue morning sky like an annunciation from on high.

"Go!" Sam shouted.

A metal fragment whined and ricocheted past Dean's ear, close enough that he felt the breeze, and he ducked belatedly, grim-faced. The next one could just as easily take his head off, he knew.

The engine was still picking up speed. It would've been

faster to run.

We never would've made it.

In front of the engine, a phalanx of demons stood on the tracks, firing directly at the train as it rammed toward them. Sheriff Daniels brought the Gatling around and mowed them down. A second later the engine roared over their bodies, spitting out gobbets of flesh and shredded uniforms beneath the wheels.

Dean didn't even see them. His eyes were nailed to the church, its front steps and its front door.

Two blocks now.

Closing in.

Get ready.

"Sam!" he shouted.

When Dean hit the brakes again, his brother was positioned halfway back in the coal car, clutching the sides, headed for the flatcar.

"Take the sheriff with you," Sam called up. "I'll stay here and try to hold them off as long as—"

His toe struck something soft. The words broke off in his throat, and he stared down at the body in the coal car. Something opened up in the pit of his stomach, hollow and quavering, as if he'd gone plunging downward.

The body of Sarah Rafferty lay motionless at his feet, her upturned eyes half-open, glassy. A bullet had struck her chest, creating a small red splotch that stained her blouse between her breasts, no bigger than a silver dollar. Beneath her, the stain was much bigger, and Sam realized that he was standing in a pool of her blood.

"Oh no…" Dean was shaking his head. "Is she…?"

Sam looked at his brother. He opened his mouth and closed it. When he spoke finally, his voice didn't sound as if it belonged to him.

"Go." Stepping over Sarah's body, he got to the Gatling gun and touched Sheriff Daniels' arm. "You have the last coil of the noose?"

She held it up.

"Right here."

"Go with Dean."

Daniels stepped out and Sam took her place, grabbing the gun's blood-slick handle and cranking it hard. Out of the corner of his eye he saw Dean and Daniels jumping off the train and running between the pillars and up the front steps of the church. Two demons jumped out from behind one of the pillars, and Sam took aim and tore them to pieces.

Dean and the sheriff disappeared inside.

Sam dropped the Gatling's crank and knelt down next to Sarah's body, dragging her as far as he could into the relative cover of the coal car. Bullets spanged and rattled everywhere.

He put his hand to her throat to feel for a pulse. She was still warm—it had only been moments.

Nothing.

"He's in here somewhere," Daniels whispered. "I can feel it."

They crossed the sanctuary, the hardwood floor creaking

faintly beneath their feet. Daniels' voice sounded small amid the cavernous emptiness. Light coming from the variegated stained-glass windows fell across her face like a succession of ever-changing moods. Dean followed after her, padding in silence between rows of empty pews leading up to the dais. The only things he felt was hurt and tired.

And oddly cold. It was unnaturally frigid beneath the high arched ceiling, as if some lost vestige of winter had stayed canned up inside, waiting for them.

"Through here," the sheriff said in a low voice.

She stopped in front of the pulpit. There was a high oak platform rising fifteen feet above them. Running her fingers along the outer edge, Daniels found what she was looking for and pressed on it. There was a click of some mechanism uncoupling, and the pulpit's front panel dropped open to reveal a dark rectangle of dusty space directly in front of them.

Crouching, she ducked through it, vanishing inside. Dean heard her and wished for a flashlight.

Then blackness swallowed him whole.

They were in a narrow passage, the walls tight enough that he could feel them on both sides, brushing against his shoulders. Off in the void, the shuffling sounds of Daniels' footfalls led him forward an inch at a time. Dean stretched his hands out in front of him, groping for something of substance and touching only air.

He crept forward.

Reaching...

And feeling something cold and tight grab him from behind.

A hand.

"There you are," McClane's voice spoke brightly in his ear, laughing. "You made it after all."

Hunched down in the coal car, Sam bent over Sarah, doing chest compressions, alternating with rescue breaths. When he pushed down on her chest, blood bubbled up from underneath her blouse.

She's dead. You can't save her.

He ignored the voice.

Kept working.

"Come on," he said, unaware that he was speaking aloud. "Come on, Sarah."

Her mouth dropped open slightly, as if she'd just remembered something she'd wanted to say. Instead, a shiny blood-bubble formed at her lips and burst, painting her lower lip with a bright smear of kabuki makeup.

Her head rolled to one side.

Footsteps rang out in the coal car behind him, and when Sam lifted his head, he saw five demons in blue and gray uniforms grinning down at him. The barrels of their muskets looked huge in his face.

"You should never have left the gun," one of them said. It drew closer.

It's up to you now, child.

Jackie Daniels came off the ladder and stepped down into the square, lead-lined room.

It was absolutely dark in here, drained of every germ of light, but that didn't matter. She knew this space by heart. The walls, floors and ceiling, and the square of dirt in the middle where the reliquary waited—these intricacies were as familiar to her as her own body. She'd been made to learn all of it when she was young, instructed by her grandfather when he'd told her of the enormous responsibility that lay before her as the next guardian of the noose.

It's up to you.

In the darkness, something clinked, dragging closer.

Daniels froze. Her scalp prickled, the sensation spreading down between her shoulder blades. Her heart sped up, pounding so hard that she could feel it in her throat. She smelled old animal skins, ancient fabric and dust.

The jingling, clinking sound grew closer.

"I brought it back," she said into the darkness, and she forced herself to take another step. She almost expected to collide with the jingling shape—that was how close it felt. "The last coil. It's here."

The jingling shape moved again. It must have heard her, but it didn't speak.

Kneeling down, she felt the damp crumbs of dirt and the cold edge of the reliquary. It was already in place—open and waiting.

She dropped the last coil inside, and snapped it shut.

For an instant nothing happened.

Then everything did.

* * *

In the darkness, McClane's laughter was very close, the sound of it horribly familiar. It smelled like sweat and burning rubber and brimstone.

"You know something?" Dean said, doing everything he could to keep his voice steady. "You know the difference between you and me? I never bent down to kiss the devil's ass."

The laughter stopped.

Dean felt the other hand land on his throat.

Not a hand.

A *claw*.

Squeezing.

The vice-grip shut his airway down instantly, and there was an almost inaudible popping sound as the cartilage began to crush inside him.

Dean's hand went to his belt, where he'd tucked the demon-killing knife, and he drew it out.

Hope you got it where it needs to go, Sheriff, he thought, and as the darkness began to spin, he plunged the blade into McClane's chest.

Even on his knees inside the coal car, Sam could see the light erupting out of the church windows, flooding the stained-glass Bible scenes from the inside and spraying the colors into the morning air. A pillar of pure white light shattered its way through the steeple and into the sky, cutting a wide bright shaft of radiance straight up into the cloudless expanse. The old planks creaked, knocking together, rattling hard. Energy shuddered and throbbed from inside, a pulsing storm of megawatt intensity, as if some silent, benevolent detonation had just occurred.

At that point Sam stopped watching.

He was more preoccupied by the demons smoking out in front of him, their muskets falling to the bottom of the coal car. The last of them collapsed with a yowling cry of anger and dismay, its black substance swirling out through its nose and mouth.

The host-bodies lay where they fell.

Some groaned and awoke, injured, confused, bleeding from the injuries to which the demons had subjected them.

Others, like the body of Sarah Rafferty, remained still.

Dean didn't just hear Tommy McClane scream—he *felt* it. He'd been prepared for the demon to flash out, but the simultaneous return of the coil to its proper resting place must have somehow amplified what happened. The demonic essence didn't just flee, it exploded.

There was a loud, moist *pop*, accompanied by a spraying sensation against the bare skin of his cheek and forehead, and the crushing pressure on his throat was gone.

Just like that.

Dean cringed. His skin was freckled with something cold and sticky, as if a balloon covered in cold syrup had burst open in front of him. The stink was familiar, rotten and nauseating—halitosis from Hell.

Then the darkness itself exploded.

Dean's hair stood up on the back of his neck, stiffening

across his forearms. The numbing crackle of ozone filled the air. His first gut-reaction was that he'd been hit by lightning, and he began to back up as quickly as he could.

The lightstorm opened up around him in every direction. It was flashing through the sanctuary in vast, booming pavilions of pure luminescence as he charged out of the open passageway, down the center aisle, and through the front door.

Sam saw his brother racing for the front steps, leaping down them all at once and landing on the sidewalk, then whirling around to watch the last of the light ebbing away inside the First Pentecostal Church of Mission's Ridge.

When it finished, he turned and looked up and down Main Street. Columns of smoke rose over the buildings, no doubt from a handful of fires that burned in various parts of town.

The demons' host-bodies lay everywhere, dangling from windows and sprawled across rooftops. Sam watched them stirring, starting to stand up, wincing and clutching their injuries. Debris littered the sidewalks, broken glass and collapsed awnings, and a layer of airborne murk that was already dissolving in the atmosphere.

Car alarms hooted and shrilled, the modern day birdsong of early morning catastrophe.

"Sammy?"

Sam climbed down, carrying Sarah's body.

"I'm sorry," Dean said.

"Where's the sheriff?"

Dean nodded back at the church. Sirens were rising up now underneath the cacophony of car alarms. Sam imagined federal investigators, government officials and television reporters, state police, more suits and uniforms than he could imagine. They would descend upon Mission's Ridge and turn it into a buzzing hornet's nest of questions and accusations and delays.

"We don't want to be here for this," he said.

"Yeah, well," Dean said, "I'm not leaving Sheriff Daniels."

"Impala's in the impound lot. Two blocks from here."

Dean brightened at the prospect of getting his car back and somehow found the strength to smile.

"I'll bring it around."

"I'll go in and look for the sheriff." Sam set Sarah's body down next to him, turned, and started toward the church.

As he did so, the front door squeaked open, and he saw Sheriff Daniels emerge from the church and into the light. Her face was glowing, almost sunburned, her eyes bright, utterly vibrant.

"Are you all right?" he asked.

She looked down at him, at first not seeming to recognize him, then out at the ruined streets of her town, the bodies of the citizens, and those who were regaining their bearings, coming out of hiding.

"Yes." Her voice was far away. "Are they gone...?"

Sam nodded. He could already hear the familiar growl of the Impala's engine making its way closer. A moment later it appeared around the corner and pulled up to the curb. Dean opened the door and climbed out. Sheriff Daniels stood looking at them.

"I guess none of us was straight with the other," Dean said.

"I suppose not," she agreed.

"My brother and I..." Sam began, and paused, unsure how to proceed. "We came because we knew there was demonic activity here. We're hunters."

The sheriff nodded.

"I'm glad you came. My job—my real job, protecting the noose—isn't easy. My family has given their lives to it. Sometimes literally." She shrugged. "I'm not used to having any help."

Sam looked over at Sarah's body.

"I wish we could have done more."

"I probably wouldn't have let you," Daniels said. "I'm used to being the only one who knows what's really going on. But it can be hard protecting everybody when you can't trust anyone."

The words seemed to weigh on Dean in particular.

"Yeah," he said, "I get that." And then, glancing back at the car, he added, "Well, we should get going."

Daniels nodded.

"My grandfather always said, there's a time for headlights and a time for rearview mirrors." She paused. "If you see your friend again, tell him I hope he finds what he's looking for."

Sam nodded. He and Dean climbed into the Impala. The sheriff stood at the curb, watching them drive away.

EPILOGUE

After the Civil War was over, the world watched the South's long Reconstruction through newspapers and eyewitness reports and telegraphs. It was perhaps appropriate, then, that Sam and Dean Winchester watched the reconstruction of Mission's Ridge on TV in St. Mary's Medical Center in Athens, Georgia.

Dean's most fervent wish, that the hospital's cafeteria food would at least be decent, proved to be relevant—they didn't leave there for almost two days.

Mission's Ridge was on every channel, local and national. The town was still in flames, figuratively if not literally. In the wake of what had happened, investigators and the media were discussing everything from bioterrorism to mass hallucination to religious hysteria. All the usual analysts, crisis experts, and pundits were brought in to comment.

Larger discussions of the Civil War, Southern culture, and racism loomed large in the background, and Dean Winchester, who tended to think about "big themes" the same way that alcoholics think about hangovers, stopped listening.

But still he watched.

Sitting out in the waiting room, looking at the screen, he saw Sheriff Jacqueline Daniels talking to reporters from the steps in front of her office, patiently answering questions and proffering explanations. She didn't seem worried. She looked calm and utterly professional.

Yet every so often Dean would see something in her eyes, a flicker of deeper recognition, as if she somehow knew he was out here, fifty miles away, watching her on TV.

Nah, she's got bigger fish to fry, he mused. *Besides, she was a real tough cookie.*

He wondered what it might be like if he could drive back to the Ridge one more time, catch her in between interviews, take her out for a beer and a bump. Would a woman like that drink whiskey? Dean had no doubt that she would.

Give it up. Put her on the list. Ones that got away.

"Hey."

He looked over and saw Sam standing next to him. The bandage on Sam's face looked white, clean and entirely out of place.

"Ready to go?"

"Yeah."

* * *

They walked back through the waiting area, out of the door toward the parking lot where the Impala was waiting. It was a perfect afternoon in late spring, cloudless, and Sam could smell the live oak. He glanced up to see a familiar figure standing next to the car waiting for them.

"Cass," Dean said. "Sorry again about the whole Witness thing."

Castiel looked away without comment.

"Did you ever talk to him?" Sam asked. "To Judas?"

"Yes." Castiel appeared even more dour than usual, as if pressed down by some burden so heavy that he alone could measure its weight. "Enough to..."

He let the words trail off with a shrug.

"Can we give you a ride or something?" Dean asked.

The angel shook his head.

"I've made other arrangements."

"So you just dropped by to bum us out?" Dean asked. "Make us feel bad for surviving another go-round with evil incarnate? You want me to buy you a balloon or something? How about a beer?"

"A beer?"

"You've heard of that—I bought you one before. And there's a place not far from here. I'm ready for a brewskie myself." Dean looked at Sam. "Come on, what do you say? I bet they have Bad Company on the jukebox."

Castiel faced them gravely.

"Those demons were organized. They had a plan, and access to a relic against which we had almost no defense, and they fully expected to force Sam into becoming Lucifer's vessel. These days are darker than ever." His gaze was dark, galvanic with foreboding. "What happened in Mission's Ridge was more than some freak incident. With the Apocalypse imminent, it was indication of things to come."

"Look, Cass..." Dean started, and the rest of the words trailed away. *I might as well be talking to empty space.* He shook his head. "Great."

"Come on," Sam said to his brother. "Get in."

They got in the Impala and Dean started the engine, pulling out of the parking lot and driving toward town. The bar they ended up at was called the Stars and Bars, and although there was indeed beer and Bad Company on the jukebox, they didn't stay long—they drank their drinks and moved on.

By seven o'clock in the evening they were back on the highway, heading north. Sam was still thinking about Sarah, but he left the great state of Georgia with few regrets.

Sheriff Daniels was right, he realized.

There is a time for headlights and a time for rearview mirrors.

Tonight, that was good enough for him.

THE END

ACKNOWLEDGMENTS

Although this manuscript was edited on a book tour in hotel rooms and airports across the country, I wrote the first draft in my basement, under the tightest deadline of my life—a little over three weeks. It simply couldn't have happened without Christopher Cerasi at DC Comics and Cath Trechman at Titan Books, two terrific individuals and tireless, top-notch editors who gave me great notes and encouragement along the way. And thanks, of course, to Eric Kripke, Rebecca Dessertine and all the creative staff of *Supernatural* for creating a universe worth falling in love with in the first place.

I'm also grateful to my coworkers at Penn State Milton S. Hershey Medical Center, particularly Senior Technologist Dana Fortney, whose creative scheduling allowed me to somehow keep my full-time status while I was doing all this.

Finally, as always, I must reserve my greatest thanks for my wife Christina and my kids. They walked the battlefields of Gettysburg with me, and far more important, they continue to tolerate my antics in the basement, way past any logical reason.

ABOUT THE AUTHOR

Joe Schreiber is the author of three original horror novels: *Chasing the Dead*, *Eat the Dark*, and *No Doors, No Windows*, as well as the standalone *Star Wars* novel *Death Troopers*.

He was born in Michigan but spent his formative years in Alaska, Wyoming, and Northern California. He lives in central Pennsylvania with his wife and two young children. When he is not writing, he passes the extra hours working the midnight shift as an MRI tech in Hershey, PA. Find out more about Joe by visiting his blog:

scaryparent.blogspot.com

ALSO AVAILABLE FROM TITAN BOOKS

SUPERNATURAL
HEART OF THE DRAGON
By Keith R.A. DeCandido

When renegade angel Castiel alerts Sam and Dean to a
series of particularly brutal killings in San Francisco's
Chinatown, they realize the Heart of the Dragon is back.

SUPERNATURAL
WAR OF THE SONS
By Rebecca Dessertine & David Reed

On the hunt for Lucifer, the boys find themselves in a
small town in South Dakota where they meet Don, an
angel with a proposition, who sends them a very long way
from home.

SUPERNATURAL
ONE YEAR GONE
By Rebecca Dessertine

Dean believes that Sam is in Hell so he is trying to live a
normal life with Lisa and Ben. But when he finds a spell that
might raise Lucifer and therefore Sam, he has to investigate.

TITANBOOKS.COM

ALSO AVAILABLE FROM TITAN BOOKS

SUPERNATURAL
COYOTE'S KISS
By Christa Faust

A truck full of illegal Mexican immigrants, slaughtered
with supernatural force, is found by the side of a road.
When Sam and Dean investigate, they are plunged into a
whole new world of monsters.

SUPERNATURAL
NIGHT TERROR
By John Passarella

A speeding car with no driver, a homeless man pursued
by a massive Gila monster—it all sounds like the stuff
of nightmares. The boys realize that sometimes the
nightmares don't go away, even when you're awake.

SUPERNATURAL
FRESH MEAT
By Alice Henderson

A rash of strange deaths in the Tahoe National Forest
bring Sam, Dean and Bobby to the Sierra Nevada
mountains to hunt a monster with a taste for human flesh.

TITANBOOKS.COM